WORST FEARS

FAY WELDON

WORST FEARS

Flamingo

An Imprint of HarperCollins Publishers

Flamingo
An Imprint of HarperCollins*Publishers*
77–85 Fulham Palace Road,
Hammersmith, London w6 8jb

Published by Flamingo 1996
1 3 5 7 9 8 6 4 2

Copyright © Fay Weldon 1996

Fay Weldon asserts the moral right to
be identified as the author of this work

A catalogue record for this book
is available from the British Library

ISBN 0 00 223920 5

Set in Postscript Linotype New Baskerville by
Rowland Phototypesetting Ltd,
Bury St Edmunds, Suffolk

Printed and bound in Great Britain by
Caledonian International Book Manufacturing Ltd, Glasgow

WORST FEARS

1

'I've never seen a dead body,' said Vilna. 'Can I come too?'
'I don't see why not,' said Abbie, and they went down to the morgue together.

As Vilna and Abbie got into Abbie's little car, Diamond the labrador jumped up at Vilna. Now there was mud all over Vilna's frilly white blouse. Vilna shoved the animal away with the side of her knee-high boot and then tried to get him in the crotch with a high heel. She missed. So Diamond ran round to the driver's side and leapt up at Abbie. Abbie was wearing an old grey sweater and didn't mind. Diamond wouldn't try Vilna again: he was accustomed to animal-lovers. Vilna's rejection of him had made a great impression.

'Poor dog,' said Abbie. 'Poor dog. He's lost his master. He's bound to be upset.'

But Vilna was too busy rubbing her twisted knee to reply. With every movement Vilna jangled. A charm bracelet much loaded with chunks of gold hung from her wrist. Heavy jewelled strings fell between up-lifted breasts no longer young. She had a hooked nose, deep close-set eyes, coiffeured blonde hair and a wondrous energy best suited to the city. Abbie, on the contrary, was much at home amongst green fields and mud. She wore sneakers, jeans and an old grey sweater on which dogs' hair wouldn't show much. These were the clothes she'd worn when the call from The Cottage came. She hadn't been home to Elder House since. Neither woman wore a seat belt. Somehow a visit to the morgue forbade it. In sympathy, let them invite death.

The Cottage looked like a child's idealised drawing of home. Centre path, square garden, drive to the right, tree to the left, door in the middle, two windows flanking it, three balancing above, tiled roof with two chimneys, one on each edge. The place was built in grey local limestone, creeper-covered, and surrounded by fields. It had stood here in its present state, as a home for the gentry, for 150 years. Before that it had been a farm, before that a cottage, before that a hovel, though one mentioned in the Domesday Book, *circa* 1070 A.D.

Alexandra, the widow, sat without moving on the edge of the brass bed in the marital bedroom upstairs and stared into space. She had been like this for two hours. The space she stared into was framed by fine tendrils of Virginia creeper which had driven in between window sash and frame, and neatly quartered by the bars which contained the window panes. The old glass had survived in all four quarters: it was thin, valuable, glittery, uneven, and probably mid-Victorian. Alexandra could see the duck pond, and Diamond racing after Abbie's car to the top of the drive where it met the road to Eddon Gurney. Whether Diamond ran into the road and was killed, or not, seemed of no consequence. As it happened Diamond stopped, and lived.

Alexandra sat in suspension. She had a vision of herself as a particle in a test-tube of viscous liquid which drifted neither up nor down, but was obliged by the laws of nature to stay exactly where it was. She found it was easier to have an idea of herself as something inorganic than organic. This was Tuesday afternoon. Ned had died on the Saturday night. Alexandra had not been there when he died. She had been in London, 130 miles away, recovering from an evening on stage, as Nora in Ibsen's *A Doll's House*. Since then, wherever she was, Alexandra had been drifting in and out of this state of suspension. She supposed it was shock.

Alexandra, exhausted by this spasm of self-awareness, actually stopped sitting on the bed and lay down upon it.

Here, for twelve years, she had been accustomed to lying naked next to Ned, his warmth against hers. When they went to bed she would be cold and he would be hot. When they woke in the morning their temperatures would have evened out, so she could scarcely tell her body from his, nor wanted to.

She did not lie for long. The mattress felt uncomfortable beneath her shoulders. Perhaps a spring had gone. She got up and went to the bathroom. She could tell she was feeling better, but the improvement hurt, just as blood will when it returns to de-constricted limbs.

Her face in the mirror didn't look too bad, just rather lopsided and like her mother's. But she knew the mirror was unduly flattering. The glass was mercury-based and dated perhaps from 1790: the surface was agreeably blotched and crazed, and rewarded anyone who looked into it with its kind opinion.

Ned and she would look in it together and he would put his arm round hers and say, 'What a divine couple.' No more. She would not find his like again. Alexandra was trying not to cry too much because she was meant to be back on stage a week today. Torvald would have to call her his 'little lark' and she would have to give a convincing impression of a lark-like Nora, no matter what her personal circumstances. So much professionalism demanded. *A Doll's House* was enjoying an unexpected success and an unexpectedly long run: eight months to date.

Diamond came pounding upstairs, where he was not allowed and seldom came. He jumped up on to the brass bed and folded himself into a sulky ball. Alexandra went after him to drag him down. He went limp and stubborn, like some protester the police were trying forcibly to remove. Alexandra persisted and succeeded. Diamond skulked downstairs. He growled at Alexandra as he went, which was unusual.

The bed had never been broad enough for Alexandra's tastes.

3

She liked a wide, wide mattress on which you could lie at any angle, but Ned liked her lying close, so she put up with its narrowness. The bed was a fine piece, probably 1820s, its brass ends finely wrought and curlicued. It had, fortuitously, been left behind by the previous occupants of The Cottage, as this large house was known locally in remembrance of centuries past.

Perhaps the bed had not been so much left-behind as deliberately never-collected. The couple who last slept in it had died in hospital within a week of one another. He was ninety-seven, she ninety-four. Their heirs had despised anything old. At least the old folk had not died in the bed itself. Though since in an old house every room you lived in had probably had someone die in it and every old chair you bought from an antique shop had witnessed some dire event, what did it really matter if they had? Life drifted away from everything in the end.

They'd changed the mattress for a new one all the same, but kept the high wooden base, and Ned and Alexandra lay unfashionably but comfortably close at night. A pity if now a spring in that mattress had gone.

Abbie had changed the sheets before Alexandra arrived home from the London flat where she, Alexandra, stayed while working. Abbie had even put the dirty sheets through the washing machine. They'd been hanging on the line in the back garden by Sunday midday, which was when Alexandra had got back home. She'd noticed them flapping greenly in the wind amongst the tall artichoke plants.

The corpse was already gone by the time she arrived. She'd been both sorry and glad about that. The body had been taken off for an autopsy: compulsory, since Ned had not seen his doctor within the previous three months. If the ambulance hadn't taken the body when it did, there would have been a twenty-four hour delay before it could call again. Dr Moebius, summoned by Abbie, had made the decision the body should go when it could

4

and not hang about to wait for Alexandra's return. Alexandra had missed the body's departure by five or so minutes.

Later on Sunday Abbie had taken the green sheets from the line, folded them, and put them back in the linen cupboard, having already made up the marital bed in candy-striped blue and white. Abbie had a domestic nature, apparently undisturbed by sudden and tragic events. Alexandra wished Abbie had left the sheets alone. They would have smelt of Ned, not fabric-softener as the striped ones did. But other people, plunging about in one's linen shelves, seldom make the right decision.

Alexandra went down to the kitchen, glad to find that the house was empty. Between Sunday and Tuesday Abbie had rendered the whole house spotless. While others mourned and tore their hair, Abbie cleaned. Now there was a note on the white scrubbed table – a solid block of bleached elm, *circa* 1880, rough-hewn, with a slab base, originally used as a laundry table. It read: 'Mr Lightfoot called from the mortuary. Ned's body has just arrived back, so we are going down to have a look. Didn't want to disturb you sleeping. Try to eat something. Abbie.'

'We?' Abbie and Vilna? Surely not. Alexandra didn't mind Abbie viewing Ned's body before she did. Abbie was a good if bossy friend. It was Abbie who had called the doctor and ambulance in the early hours of the morning. Everyone had thought Ned might be still alive but actually he was dead. No doubt Abbie had gone along to the morgue now to make sure all the arrange-ments were suitable: that nothing would upset Alexandra that didn't have to. Perhaps she meant to see that the slab on which Ned lay was properly clean? In any case, Abbie had already seen the body, lying in the dining room, where Ned had apparently fallen in the throes of his heart attack. Abbie had been the very first to see it. Why shouldn't Abbie continue to communicate with the corpse if it made her feel better?

But Vilna? Alexandra didn't like the thought of Vilna viewing Ned's body before she, the wife, had done so. In fact, she didn't

5

want Vilna to see Ned dead at all. Ned scarcely knew Vilna. What he did know he didn't like. Alexandra would say, 'Oh, Vilna's OK, just highly-strung and un-English.' Ned would say, 'She's voracious. She's a monster.' Alexandra could see that Ned had been right about Vilna all along. She had hung around The Cottage ever since the news broke, like a vulture. In fact, thought Alexandra now, Vilna looked like a cross between a vulture and Ivana Trump. If Ned on his slab suddenly opened his eyes and saw Vilna and not Alexandra, who looked like a cross between a flamingo and Marilyn Monroe, he would be displeased.

2

In the morgue, Abbie and Vilna stared down at Ned's body.

> '*I went down to St James' Infirmary,*'

sang Vilna in her croaky voice.

> '*For to see my true love there.*
> *All laid out on a white table*
> *So cold, so white, so bare.*'

They stood a little distance from the body. There was full sunshine outside, but the morgue, a plain concrete structure, was windowless, very cold and artificially lit.

'Ned liked me to sing,' Vilna observed. 'I have a very fine voice, don't you think?'
'Very fine,' said Abbie.

'He looks younger now he's dead,' said Vilna.
'Do you think so?' asked Abbie, politely.
'Definitely,' said Vilna. She had a middle-European drawl. She lengthened the vowels and thickened the consonants. It was as if the earthy spirit of her cunt rose up to issue from her mouth. 'He's a very handsome man, don't you think?' said Vilna, and stretched out her hand to touch the bare, strong, muscled, cold, marble forearm. 'Especially now that everything's kind of tautened up around his chin.'
'Was,' said Abbie. 'Not is. And I don't think you should touch him.'

7

'You English,' said Vilna. 'So inhibited! So cut off from proper emotion.'

Vilna moved to stand next to the corpse, and pulled back the sheet that reached to mid-chest. Ned was wearing a white T-shirt and a pair of thin white cotton trousers, tightened and tied in a bow with a cloth drawstring. Vilna undid the bow, loosened the string and, ignoring the fly, simply turned the fine fabric back. Now they could see the crudely sewn autopsy scar which reached almost to the crotch. The penis lay dormant, firm and thick, as if carved in stone, part of the whole.

'He's only forty-nine,' said Vilna, 'and so good at it. What a waste!'
'*Was* only forty-nine,' said Abbie.
'He doesn't look at all dead to me,' said Vilna.
Abbie got the better of her natural abhorrence at touching anything dead. She refastened the trousers. She pulled the sheet up to Ned's chest. Someone had to. Vilna couldn't be allowed to run riot.

Ned was the morgue's only occupant. The place was situated in the yard of the undertaker's office, where the ceremonial hearses were parked. The morgue's shop-front faced directly on to the curve of Gurney's High Street where the pavement narrowed almost to non-existence. There was an urn in the window containing dried flowers, and some dead flies trapped between the double-glazing. The front door had a nice little Georgian portico often pointed out to visitors to the town, but it was hard to open. Most clients used the side door. Who, in any case, wanted to be observed as they went in and out, going about their dismal business? The vehicle used for transporting corpses – 'Private Ambulance – Lightfoot and Sons' – was parked outside the porch, in the street, creating a traffic hazard on a blind curve. Few people understood why it was there, or what it was used for.

'You're interested in the Roman cemetery,' said Mr Lightfoot

8

to Abbie as she emerged into the sun to wait for Vilna. The cold had got to her bones. 'Tell your friends in the Bohemian Belt that I had a bagful of bones from the University today. Returned from the Roman cemetery excavation. The Bishop is coming to inter the remains with the dignity they deserve.'

Mr Lightfoot was gaunt and thin and pale, as if he often went underground himself, in sympathy with his clients. People would pay him in advance, for fear their families would skimp on the funeral the better to prosper themselves.

'I'm glad to hear that,' said Abbie. 'I'm glad to know he can finally overlook the fact that those are pagan and not Christian bones.'

'I hope you lot turn up for the ceremony,' said Mr Lightfoot, 'after the fuss you conservationists made. What this town needs is development, not undisturbed remains.'

'Of course we'll turn up,' said Abbie. 'Those of us who remain.' Ned had been prime mover in the 'Save the Roman Cemetery' campaign.

'Makes no difference to me,' said Mr Lightfoot, 'if a person dies now or two thousand years ago. I agree with you: any corpse deserves the best. Mind you, I wouldn't be saying the University sent back exactly the same bones as they took. Any old bones, any old period, they look like to me, from the back of any old curator's shelf. But human, decidedly human. It's the gesture that counts.'

Abbie and Vilna got into the car, unwilling to converse on such a subject at such a time.

'Will Mrs Ludd be coming to view the body?' asked Mr Lightfoot.

'All in good time,' said Abbie. 'Is the temperature in there low enough?'

'I'll be the best judge of that,' said Mr Lightfoot. 'It's customary that the first ones to view a body are the widow and the children, if any. I was surprised to see you two come up. But I expect you do things differently in the Bohemian Belt: you see the body in an artistic light.'

'We do the best we can,' said Abbie, 'to deal with grief; like everyone else.'

9

'Darling, do let's get out of this doomy place,' said Vilna, loud enough for Mr Lightfoot to hear. 'Everyone hereabouts is quite, quite mad.'

Abbie manoeuvred the car backwards out of the yard. She was being harassed by Vilna; the Private Ambulance obscured her view of the road; she all but collided with a little hatchback coming into the yard. In the passenger seat, haggard, tear-stained and aghast, was a dumpy middle-aged woman. A white-haired man neither Vilna nor Abbie recognised was driving. His face was set and grim.

Abbie regained control of the car.
'I've cricked my neck, darling,' said Vilna. 'You should be more careful.'
'But did you see who that was?' asked Abbie.
'It was Jenny,' said Vilna. 'Of course.'

3

When Abbie and Vilna got back to The Cottage, Alexandra was weeding the pansies in the back garden as if nothing had happened. Diamond sat upright on the low stone wall which kept the rampant foliage of the back garden from falling into the house and allowed access to the back door to guests, milkman and canvassers alike. The front door was large and stiff, the path to it not in good condition, so it was seldom used: the back door did instead.

'Was Ned all right?' Alexandra asked Abbie. She looked through and beyond Vilna.
'He was just fine,' said Abbie.
Vilna snorted and said she must be off. She'd taken a chill. She should have known you'd need a jacket in a morgue. Could Abbie give her a lift back?

Abbie said she'd stay another night if Alexandra wanted. Alexandra said no, she was OK now. She could be on her own. Sooner or later you had to cope with the ghosts. Ned's brother would be coming the next day. Abbie's own family would need her.

Abbie asked if Alexandra wanted her to come with her when she went to see the body, and Alexandra said she'd go down on her own in good time: she expected even a body needed some rest from constant observation.

Vilna said, as their car drove away:

'She was gardening without gloves. Can you believe that? One of our leading actresses? She'll ruin her hands.'

'Actor,' said Abbie, but Vilna did not take the point.

Abbie had left the answerphone on. This meant, Alexandra realised, that whoever called would hear Ned's voice on the tape. She went into Ned's study and used the office phone to call the house and listened to Ned's voice herself. She said in reply, 'Hi, Ned, this is me,' and hung up. She looked for the instruction booklet which would tell her how to change the tape, but failed to find it. She solved the problem by removing the phone jack from the wall. She did not wish to erase the tape in case Sascha, now four, wanted to hear what his father's voice sounded like when he grew up. Except, of course, perhaps Sascha wouldn't. Always a disappointment to have Gods turned into mortals. Who ever enjoyed hearing Einstein's voice on CD Rom and realising he was just another old man?

Alexandra removed the more disturbing memories of Ned from the living room: a pair of his shoes, the proof of the critical essay on Ibsen he had been writing and hoping to finish at the weekend. She glanced at a column or two: apparently Ned found *A Doll's House* the worst constructed and most sentimental of Ibsen's works. Shoes and papers went into a cupboard to wait until she was prepared to face the job of clearing the evidence of his life away in a proper fashion. She ejected the tape from the video machine. Ned had apparently pressed 'Stop' some ten minutes into *Casablanca*. Why *Casablanca*? She, Alexandra, was the one who so admired Bogart. Ned would dismiss him as a performer rather than an actor. What had induced Ned to watch Bogart on a Saturday night? He could never tell her. She would never know.

Alexandra sat on the arm of the sofa and stared again at nothing in particular. She supposed this now familiar state of suspension served as some sort of absorption buffer for emotion: it was a drifting, waking sleep. It was not pleasant: on the contrary; but at least while she was in it unpleasant thoughts travelled in a loop, round and round, so you got immune to them. They did not branch out into anything different or worse. She imagined that an animal in a bad situation, caught in a trap, in a vivisection lab, lost and hungry, would feel no worse than this. If you had a poor memory, no language skills, very little sense of time, and a limited understanding of cause and effect, this was what it would be like. Buffered by these constraints, you would not suffer too much.

Alexandra's hand went to sleep. She'd been sitting on it. She stood up and shook her arm until the blood returned. It was dark outside. The house seemed alive with unnatural noise. Bangings and creakings came from upstairs. She thought perhaps Diamond had gone up again, and went after him. On her way up the stairs she thought something invisible and unpleasant brushed past her and went ahead of her. She was terrified but went on. She stood at the top of the stairs and listened. Nothing. If anything, everything was now suddenly quieter than it ought to be, as if someone was saying if you don't like noise, try quiet, see how you like that. She didn't like it, but on balance it was preferable to bangs and crashes, a sense of whisperings and the movement of invisible entities. There was no sign of Diamond. Old houses would do this, of course. She should not attribute inexplicable sounds to supernatural causes. No doubt all her senses were unduly edgy.

Plumbing would echo through the wooden structure of an old house as referred pain did through the body. Impeded liver function, for example, would surface as a pain in the right shoulder. It had been a warm day; now it was cold: sudden changes of temperature could cause this structure, this material, to contract, that other to expand: noise could come from anywhere, just as did aches and pains.

All the same, Alexandra turned on all available lights. She even pushed open the door of her bedroom, which once had been her and Ned's bedroom, and although she didn't enter it because of the brooding presences within she slipped her hand round the door and turned on the light and went away. Now the house would glow like a beacon to anyone travelling along the top road to Eddon Gurney: we will not be defeated. The road was not much frequented these days – a new bypass siphoned off most of the heavy traffic, which was good for property prices but could make those who lived in The Cottage feel unduly isolated at the best of times. And these were not they: it was as if the here-and-now had slipped, in the aftermath of sudden death, into something shaky and incoherent.

Property prices, money, wills, insurance claims, documents, certificates: she would think about all these later in the week. There was no hurry. Hamish, Ned's brother, would help her out. While the *Doll's House* run lasted at least she had an income. Alexandra turned on all the downstairs lights as well. She went into the kitchen. Diamond was lying beneath the table and not in his basket. She thought she would stay in this room; it seeming less haunted than anywhere else in the house. She moved a chair so that when she sat her leg would be in contact with Diamond's solid warmth, but no sooner had she sat than Diamond moved away. Well, he was entitled. He had been alone with the body for hours, without help of human kind. Diamond must find her, Alexandra, neglectful and wilfully so. What did he know about the necessity of earning a living? His food just appeared in a bowl.

Abbie had put a jam jar of summer flowers from the garden on the table. They were browning and failing: they looked as if they needed water, but when Alexandra tested the level with her finger there was plenty there. Perhaps death in a house made flowers wilt sooner than they should?

Alexandra sat with her head in her arms at the kitchen table. She closed her eyes. She was on a speedboat with Ned: they were on a wide, wide lake; a white foamy wake spread out behind in the deep, still water. They were good close companions on a journey. The day was brilliant, glittery with light. The boat was making for a shore, a beach, a forest; there was a greeny-blue mountain in the background. The boat was suddenly faced with a wall of shadow: a fog. The light in front, over water, beach, forest, mountain, was washed with dark. The boat stopped a fraction before the fog began. Alexandra stayed with it, still in bright light. She remained as she was, suspended; but Ned didn't stop: he spun suddenly on into the fog. Now he stood on the shore with his back to her; he seemed puzzled, forlorn. She watched him leave the beach and plod on into the dense, dark forest. She called out after him but he didn't hear, and didn't look back. There was no helping him. She knew he was beyond help. Nor did her heart go out to him. He was alone. The vision stopped, as a film stops. She was awake, but had not been asleep in the first place. The last frame stayed in her mind, indelible. Herself on the lake, in the sunlight – Ned going on into the forest: tired, so tired, without her blessing. The vision was framed like a picture in the glitter of her own life.

Alexandra tried to dismiss the vision – for so she saw it – as created by some sort of hotch-potch in her own mind. A doomy mixture. The bourn from which no traveller returns? Whatever a bourn might be. An illustration of Walter de la Mare's 'The Traveller' in a volume she'd had as a child? The weary voyager turned away, limping on his stick, journeying on into the murk of the forest. But Alexandra could not convince herself that what she had seen was old stuff rehashed: no, it was too new, too vivid for that. Clearly fresh and framed in her mind. And the dream, or rather vision – and Alexandra could tell the difference, because she had such a clear impression of not having woken but simply of having been in a more perceptive and realer than real state before – was reassuring. She had a blueprint of what had happened, to which she could now refer. Alexandra stayed – Ned went on. Why she had made where he was going into so dire a place, she could not say. Why she had refused him her blessing she did not know. But at least she now had in her head an actual location where Ned could be. She had seen it, and was comforted.

There was an umbilical cord between them: his for her, hers

for him. It would in time pull him back; or would she follow him? Perhaps she would have another vision soon: Ned would reappear on the beach to wait for her; the cloud would be gone; she would join him on the shore in the sunlight. They'd go on into some other form of life, together. That was how it went. She could not accept the finality of death. Here now, then suddenly not here. Impossible. The line between the two states was too sharp and clear to be acceptable. Everything else drifted from one stage to another, grew, developed, faded, dispersed; why should this be different? She felt almost cheerful.

4

Alexandra, in need of conversation, plugged the phone jack back in the wall. It rang at once. During the evening there were seventeen calls.

Three people hung up as soon as she answered.

One asked for Jenny and then hung up when Alexandra said, 'Wrong number.' Alexandra felt bad for a minute, because after all it might have been for Jenny Linden, whose name was next to theirs in so many address books: Linden, Jenny; Ludd, Ned and Alexandra. Only the L-o's could intervene and there weren't too many of those. Though she'd once known a Loseley. But it was too late anyway: the callers had evaporated.

One from the theatre. Sam, the front-of-house manager, to say the understudy Daisy Longriff was atrocious, houses were bound to suffer as a result of Alexandra's absence, but there was no fear of Daisy being asked to take over the role permanently. Alexandra must just relax and not return before time.
'A whole crowd of us will want to come down to the funeral, darling,' he said. 'So long as it's in the morning, and not on a matinee day.'
Alexandra said apologetically she didn't think anyone Ned had savaged in his time – and there were many; that was the fate of critics, to make enemies – should feel obliged to come to his funeral. Sam said, 'Ned was a man of integrity. The play was always the thing. He spoke as he found. He'll be sorely and sincerely missed.'
Alexandra said, 'You mean everyone will want to come to his

funeral,' and laughed for the first time since Sunday. She explained to Sam that her brother-in-law Hamish was coming down the next day from Edinburgh to arrange everything, including funeral dates; she'd do what she could; otherwise she supposed there'd be a memorial service sometime later, in London.

'You're in your competent mood,' said Sam. 'That's better than "poor-little-me". Look on the bright side: at least you were saved from him falling dead at your feet.'

'I don't like to think of him dying alone,' said Alexandra.

Sam said, 'Why wasn't he in the London flat making you cocoa anyway?'

Alexandra said, 'He had too much work to do,' and began to cry, so Sam concluded the call.

The next call was from Irene, Alexandra's mother. She lived with her fourth husband next to a golf course in Surrey. She had Romanoff blood, way back in the past. 'How are you, darling?' she asked. 'Has Ned been back to say goodbye to you yet?' And Irene explained, as she often did, that the dead would appear in dreams to the bereaved in order of their closeness and say goodbye. Ned, she implied, was being laggardly, in death as in life.

'He's been, Mother,' said Alexandra, as diplomatic in Ned's death as she was in his life. 'I expect he was waiting until after the autopsy, when he could settle.'

'I'd rather not think about that,' said Irene. 'As for Sascha, he's just fine. Don't worry about him. I'll keep him here till you're ready.'

Alexandra had been to her mother's to see Sascha on the Saturday afternoon. She had expected Ned to bring the child up to London at the weekend as usual, after nursery school. Then, apart from Saturday night, they'd have the weekend together as a family. Instead Ned had taken Sascha to Irene's on Thursday and left him there, claiming pressure of work. He'd gone back home and two days later died, around midnight, ten minutes into *Casablanca*.

'But I want Sascha with me,' said Alexandra. 'I need him. He's my child.'

'I daresay you do need him,' said Irene, 'but what does little Sascha need? He needs a cheerful mother, an organised home, and proper child care while you're at work. So I'll keep him till you've got your act together, if you don't mind, in his interests not yours.'

'But I have to tell him his father's dead,' said the daughter.

'What's the hurry?' enquired the mother.

'Shouldn't one tell a child at once?' asked Alexandra. 'Won't he find out?'

'Not if he can't read the papers,' snapped her mother. 'Because I'm certainly not going to tell him.'

Alexandra recalled how the news of her own father's death had been kept from her for a week or more, till Irene felt strong enough to tell her. She had always resented it. A similar fate was being prepared for Sascha.

'OK,' said Alexandra. She was exhausted. Perhaps after she had talked to Hamish tomorrow she would simply drive all the way to Sussex and pick up Sascha. The child care, Theresa, wasn't yet back from holiday, but that hardly mattered now.

It seemed unlikely that Alexandra would be back to work by the following Tuesday. She supposed, speculatively, that it would be possible to back out of the production altogether. They would hardly hold her to her contract. Daisy Longriff might yet get the part of Nora on a permanent basis. It occurred to Alexandra that Longriff would come between Linden and Ludd in an address book.

'Alexandra,' said Irene. 'Now I don't want to upset you, you're upset enough already: but there's something strange going on here.'

'What?' asked Alexandra. She felt bad-tempered as well as tired. Her mother was convinced, as mothers often are whose own lives are not above suspicion, that Ned was unfaithful to her daughter. Alexandra could explain and explain that these days men could have women friends and women men friends without any sexual sub-text, but Irene would have none of it.

'What time did Abbie call you?'

'Six in the morning,' said Alexandra. 'From the house. It took me two hours to get over the shock, and I drove down on my own which I shouldn't have, and ran out of petrol and didn't arrive till twelve, and the ambulance had just taken the body away. It was terrible.'

'Poor Alexi,' said Irene, in the soothing mother's voice which at the best of times made Alexandra want to cry. 'You still won't see it. What was Abbie doing at The Cottage at six in the morning? More like half past five, because it seems she called the doctor before she called you.'

'Jesus,' said Alexandra, 'I don't know. Mushrooming; leaving edible fungi at Ned's door. Taking her students out to look at an English dawn. Needing a telephone: the students are always *en crise.* Whatever.'

'Darling,' said Irene. 'You're in denial.'

Alexandra slammed the phone down. It buzzed again.

Dr Moebius said, 'I've been trying to get through to you for hours, Mrs Ludd. There's either no reply or the line's busy. Now it's very late.'

'There's always tomorrow morning,' said Alexandra, with a temper better reserved for her mother. 'What's your hurry? People are a long time dead.'

'It was you I was concerned about,' said Dr Moebius, a little stiffly. 'I have not seen you since your husband died.' Dr Moebius headed the local Health Centre. He was known to be a pleasant man, a bad diagnostician, and gullible; much given to acts of faith. He was as likely to recommend acupuncture as surgery, meditation as medication. He was a favourite with terminally ill patients, who looked forward to having him at their death beds. He would pray, and believed in heaven.

'I could do with some sleeping pills,' said Alexandra. She had searched out the carton in the bathroom cabinet but found it empty. She'd remembered it with at least eight tablets left. Perhaps Ned had needed them, in her absence.

'Not a good idea,' said Dr Moebius. 'Lime tea's just as efficacious and easier on the liver. I wanted to tell you the autopsy report

20

is in. Massive myocardial infarction; a heart attack, in layman's terms. What we all supposed. Unfortunately the forensic people have only done half of what I required, so the body has had to go back to them. Technically I should have asked your permission first, but Mr Lightfoot's ambulance was on its way back to the lab, empty –'

'You wouldn't want to waste the opportunity, I can see,' said Alexandra. 'But if my husband died of a heart attack, isn't that all you need to know?'

'That's not the point,' said Dr Moebius. 'The labs take liberties. I asked for a brain dissection – there was a possibility of cerebral haemorrhage. It was not the lab's decision to take. They cut corners. You've already viewed the body, in any case.'

'I have not,' said Alexandra.

'Oh,' said Dr Moebius. 'Mr Lightfoot said you had.'

It seemed perfectly possible to Alexandra that Mr Lightfoot was right. What did she know? She was only the wife.

No sooner had that call finished, when her mother was back on the line.

'Don't worry about it,' said Irene. 'I'm not offended. I know how upset you are and how difficult for you this is. But why haven't you asked Abbie what she was doing at The Cottage at five in the morning?'

'Six.'

'Half past five,' conceded Irene. 'Well? Isn't it an obvious thing to ask? How can you deny you're in denial?'

'But one would, wouldn't one?' remarked Alexandra. There was such a sharp dividing line between the world in which Ned was alive and the world in which Ned wasn't, there seemed something indecent in trying to link the two. 'And then Ned died,' was like a tidal wave which swept through your dining room carrying everything before it, flinging all familiar bits and pieces everywhere, snapping and sheering in its violent onward rush. To try and retrieve and piece together this one mingy little detail seemed almost impolite. Had he been frightened? Or was it all too sudden? Did he gasp for air, look round for help and find her not there? Ten minutes into *Casablanca*? What could he have

21

found so upsetting in *Casablanca*? Did one need to be upset to have a heart attack? Or did it just happen? He'd switched the video off: had he walked about the house feeling uneasy, searching for breathing air?

'Darling,' said Irene, 'are you OK?'

'Things just suddenly hit me,' said Alexandra. 'Sorry.'

'People are like quarks, darling,' said Irene from her house at the edge of the golf course. 'They wink out of one part of this universe and wink in somewhere else, simultaneously.'

'You're optimistic. Ned's plodding up a hill somewhere,' said Alexandra bleakly, 'in a hideous, doomy fog, and I can't help him.'

But she told her mother she'd ask Abbie for more detail, and her mother went away.

The next call was from David, a colleague of Ned's. He was weeping and incoherent. He'd only just heard the news. Alexandra was sympathetic and comforting, but she held the phone a long way away from her ear.

When David had gone, Alexandra called Abbie.

'Abbie,' she said, 'my mother wants to know. What were you doing in my house at half past five in the morning?'

'I'd had a row with Arthur,' said Abbie, as if she had been waiting for the question. 'I'd gone for a drive to calm myself; I was driving along the main road; I could see The Cottage with every light blazing. I thought Ned was in London: he usually is at weekends: I went down to see what was going on, in case it was burglars. I looked through the dining-room window and saw Ned on the floor, so I went on in. The door wasn't locked. You never lock your doors. You're too trusting. OK? I wondered when you'd ask.'

'It's just my mother wanted to know,' repeated Alexandra.

'That figures,' said Abbie. 'She doesn't miss a thing.'

'Why do you think Ned turned all the lights on?' asked Alexandra.

'I have no idea,' said Abbie. 'Why don't you try to sleep, Alexandra? I'll come over if you like.'

'I'm just fine,' said Alexandra. She thought Abbie's answer was rather pat. It sounded rehearsed. But then it would be. How did pathologists get into a skull to examine a brain? Anything but think of that.

5

Abbie said to Arthur: 'I don't think she believed me.'
Arthur said to Abbie: 'It's just as well. She has to find out sooner or later. She has to know. Can we forget Alexandra and can you take some notice of me?'
Abbie said to Arthur: 'Why does she have to know? What are friends for? Not to speak the truth, that's for sure.'

Arthur covered her mouth with his hand. They were rolling about on the heavy old bed in marital bliss. The sheets were white, starched and ironed. Abbie and Arthur lived in Elder House, an old rectory next to a disused church a couple of miles from The Cottage. The church bell still hung in its tower and on stormy nights, depending on the way of the wind, it would suddenly peal out. Then students from many lands would run out into the corridors of Elder House in terror of ghosts and spirits. Arthur and Abbie would calm them. In the morning over the breakfast table Abbie would read them the scene in *Jane Eyre* where Miss Ingram and her friends, roused by the mad wife's shrieks, run out into the corridors and encounter Jane, flitting about in her white nightie. The students would eat their traditional English breakfast – sausage, bacon, egg, mushrooms – while they listened. Impressed by their own reactions, they would sign up for yet another course. These were experiences to last them all their lives. Arthur and Abbie would just have a little fruit, a little yoghurt, and some black coffee. They could have had the bell removed easily enough, or de-gonged as a dog is de-barked, but preferred not to.

Abbie and Arthur ran a residential school for would-be English teachers from foreign lands. Bored with teaching, they went on teaching. They had no choice. They could not sell Elder House – no one wanted it – so they made the best of what they had. They were good at that: a stoical couple.

Presently they slept. Downstairs the help still laboured, laying-up for breakfast, clearing away the students' late-night coffee and biscuits. She was lucky to have the job. The countryside is pretty, Arthur would say, because there are so few people in it, and the reason there are so few people is because there are so few jobs.

Abbie went into a cave and saw Ned behind a pane of glass, smiling at her. He sat on a rock like a merman. His legs had fused into a tail. Waves lapped up against the glass. She waved. He waved back. Abbie moved on, as if she were in an aquarium and there was something more interesting to see further on. It was a casual encounter, like a one-night stand.

Abbie woke Arthur and told him what she had seen.
'Ned won't like having a tail,' said Arthur. 'No chance of a leg-over now.' He went back to sleep.
'It wasn't a dream,' said Abbie. 'It was a vision. I woke up before I had it.'
She woke Arthur again.
'All that wailing and screaming on Saturday night, all that com-motion,' she complained. 'Ned being dead was the least part of it. Even calling the ambulance was just to keep Jenny quiet. The reason I went to see the body was to convince myself he was dead.'
'Did it?'
'No,' said Abbie. 'Not at the time. I believe it now I've seen him in the aquarium. He's in a different place from ours.'
She began to cry. Arthur woke up enough to comfort her.
'You're something,' he said. 'Try and either wake up or go to sleep.' She woke up.
'And what did Vilna mean by saying Ned was so good at it? What

25

does Vilna know?' demanded Abbie. 'She's a monster. She's competing for the status of most-bereaved. She's the kind who moves in after a death and squabbles over who's the closest, who's suffering most. It's disgusting. She's ghoulish.'

'If she's a monster and a ghoul,' said Arthur, 'why have her as a friend?'

'Because there are so few people round here to talk to,' complained Abbie, and fell asleep. He, of course, could not.

6

Morning. With Ned not there Alexandra could stretch across the bed. She took what consolation she could from this. Nor was Sascha there to stalk into the bedroom, as was his habit, with his straight back, curly blond hair and censorious blue eyes, to start the day earlier than either she or Ned wanted. She must learn to extract Ned from these sorts of mental equations. *Erratum*: earlier than *she* wanted, drop the Ned. A kind of chilliness crept in from the periphery of the bed. What would she do for sex now? What had she done before she was married? She could hardly remember. Sex, it seemed, was as forgettable as a dinner out; set-asideable as a floppy disc. Relationships got remembered: they were there on the hard disc. Alexandra had the feeling Ned lay on top of her, forbidding such thoughts: a heavy but intangible weight: a consolation. They had been married for twelve years: fifty-two weeks in the year, sex on an average, she supposed, of three times a week. Rather less lately, since *A Doll's House* had disrupted their lives but paid off the overdraft; but then more often at the beginning of the relationship to outweigh that. Five times a week, say, in the first two years before they were married; four times a week after that – marriage did seem to have a dampening effect; five to six times during late pregnancy – pregnancy, for her, did the opposite. Twice a week, even once a week, in the months after Sascha's birth – three times a week on average seemed a good but conservative bet. Twelve times three times fifty-two fucks. One thousand eight hundred and seventy-two. Jesus. No wonder, on the most basic level, she now felt bereft. And never once with a condom. How much of Ned had she not absorbed, literally? The broken spring was there again, between her shoulder-blades.

Alexandra heard a kind of keening noise outside. The bed no longer tempted her. She went to the window and looked out over the garden, the hedge, the field beyond, the duck pond. Early-morning light made everything glittery, almost too bright to see clearly. Downstairs Diamond began to bark. She could see a figure lurking just beyond the hedge: someone was skulking, and wailing. She saw, as so often in the last few days, but did not absorb. The real world ran like a TV film you watched or didn't watch, fitfully, according to mood.

Alexandra thought bereavement was like bonding: you grieved for the dead as you bonded with a newborn baby. There wasn't much you could do about either. The response was bred into you; it was genetically determined, physiological, beyond your control. If a spouse died, or a parent, a child, a sibling, or to a lesser extent when a friend or colleague died, or to a greater extent again a king, a president, a pop star or a religious leader, why then you grieved. You couldn't help it. You hurt. You stopped, just as if you had a physical pain or a fever, to wait for healing. Tears flowed. You could not even see sufficiently to act. Grief was nature's way, no doubt, of preserving the group against unnecessary death. That person did that. That person died. Don't you do it. Don't let that happen again in a hurry! Grief for the old is tempered, mild; grief for the young is acute, survival-friendly for the tribe. As is grief's companion emotion, the desire for vengeance. Hang the killers! Bomb the bombers! Sue the doctors! No further justification needed, swoop over the hill to loot, plunder, rape; steal the Sabine women, replenish the tribe. Vengeance sucks up grief, buries it. Nature's satisfied. The Gods demand human sacrifice, always did; the hideous divine maw sucks in the living, chomps down on warm flesh, kills, devours. Then healing nature gapes open its mouth and new life pours out of it, raw and writhing, an endless, ever-multiplying stream. One day it will choke on the sheer volume of its production: it has to.

More wailing from outside. A peculiar keening; an ethnic chant. Alexandra took no notice.

You had to separate out the mourning from the death. Grief was not particular to Ned. Had she married another man, and had a child by him, and he had died last Saturday night, she would be in just this same state now. Others would say, in an attempt to explain the irrationality of the emotion, 'Oh, you grieve for your own death. Another's death reminds you of your own mortality. The closer that life was, the worse it is for you.' But it wasn't necessarily so. Fear of death was reasonable: terror of the unknown, of the grim forest of non-being: but grief for oneself? No. Grief in advance for the others who in their turn will mourn you – should there be any – would be more appropriate. It was a terrible thing for anyone to be plunged without warning or their consent into mourning, but what could you lament for the dead themselves? Death came to everyone. If it came suddenly so much the better. Lucky Ned. Poor Alexandra.

Or people would say, 'Poor Ned. He won't be there to watch his child grow up.' But that didn't wash either. Children grow up to grow away. The younger the child, the purer, the more exquisite the parental feeling. Not to be there to see your child grow up would be the blessing, not the curse. It was pointless to search for reasons: grief accompanies bereavement – it is nature's stick – as joy accompanies birth – it is nature's carrot.

Grief was luxurious, in the way porridge on a cold morning is luxurious, or a cold shower on a hot day, or water when you are thirsty, or a languid kiss between lovers; anything which holds you at that pleasurable point where the satisfaction of the senses and the need for survival meet. She would go with it, not fight it. It would cure itself, as a broken leg heals itself, with a little help from friends.

The wailing and keening below was louder now; so was Diamond's barking. Just beyond the hedge, if she craned, Alexandra could see a brown hunched back moving to and fro. It seemed to be some kind of animal, roaming up and down as animals will, restless and miserable, in a confined space. But the confinement was wilful, unless the creature was on some kind of chain. And how could that be? Downstairs, trapped in the morning kitchen, Diamond hurled himself against the closed back door. He wanted out.

Alexandra dressed quickly, glad now of an occupation. Trainers, jeans, one of Ned's shirts: denim; tough, rough fabric, which partly restored the feeling that she and he were one; and went down to the kitchen. She put Diamond on the lead and went out the back door. The dog pulled and tugged her round to the front of the house, to the privet hedge which divided garden from field. A human head rose into view on its far side. It was Jenny Linden, still keening; blotched face and puffy eyes.

'What are you doing here?' asked Alexandra.
Jenny Linden stopped wailing.
'I only wanted to take the dog for a walk,' she said. She had a soft voice and a West Country lilt. She reminded Alexandra of Gollum in *The Hobbit*, a pale, white, underground thing; solid yet sinuous. Diamond wrenched the lead away from Alexandra's surprised hands, and leapt at Jenny Linden. He leapt in welcome, in friendship not hostility, and Jenny scratched him under the ears in the way Ned was accustomed to do. Alexandra never did that. She did not like dog scurf beneath her nails.

Alexandra watched as Jenny fell on her knees, embracing Diamond.
'Oh poor dog,' she cried, 'poor dog. Poor us!' Diamond licked Jenny's face with enthusiasm and Jenny let him. Presently she became aware of Alexandra staring.
'Did I wake you or something? Leah says I have to let my grief out.'
'Leah?'
'My therapist. She taught me how to keen. Didn't Ned tell you?'
'Tell me what?'
'About Leah. I suppose he wouldn't. You would have laughed. What am I going to do? I want to die.'

Her podgy face was puckered. She was in her mid-forties, older than Alexandra. Her short hair was unkempt and needed washing. She wore no make-up. She put her little white soft hand on Alexandra's lean arm, and Alexandra felt the touch like an electric shock and pulled away.

'I only came to see if I could walk Diamond,' Jenny Linden said. 'He likes to get out early. But you don't know that. You have to sleep late every morning because of the theatre.'

She raised her double chin to the heavens and wailed again. The early moon was still in the sky, palely loitering. It was a really beautiful morning, Alexandra noticed. Dew on the roses, a spiderweb glittering in the very early sunlight. Where was Ned? This was why you grieved for the dead, because they could no longer be part of the exhilaration of renewal.

'Glad that I live am I,' she sang at the other woman until she stopped her dreadful, Leah-recommended keening and stared in astonishment. Two could make a noise as well as one, and hers, Alexandra's, at least was more disciplined and had some meaning. She had hated ululation at Drama School, though she could set up as good a classic wail as anyone else. Dirges seemed mindless, and she didn't like that. She preferred a hymn, and offered one.

> *'Glad that the sky is blue*
> *Glad for the country lane*
> *Glad for the fall of dew.*
> *After the sun the rain,*
> *After the rain the sun.*
> *This be the way of life,*
> *Till the work be done.'*

'Don't be angry with me,' said Jenny Linden, though Alexandra could not see that she had displayed anger in any way. 'I'm the one you should be sorry for.'

'Why's that?' asked Alexandra.

'I loved Ned,' said Jenny, 'and he died. You didn't love him. There. I've said it.'

'You need treatment,' said Alexandra. Now she was angry. 'But

I have enough to think about at the moment, besides nutters. You'll just have to look after yourself.'

'I understand your anger,' said Jenny piously. Then her little eyes gleamed with malice. 'Ned always said you'd be angry and destructive when you found out. Dog in the manger!' she yelped, and turned and ran, little dumpy legs going one-two, one-two, little feet turning out, heavy bum jiggling, into the mists which still drifted round the foot of the poplar trees where the ground dipped. Ned and Alexandra had planted the poplars together when they first moved down to The Cottage. Twelve in a row, ten feet apart, a hard day's work, but gratifying. Diamond had already shot off in front of Jenny Linden, barking. Crows rose in response: a black spiky crowd swelling over the copper beeches which shielded the field and The Cottage from the top road. Birds of ill-omen, so plentiful round here.

Alexandra went to the kitchen and made herself some coffee. The old packet was now finished. She threw it in the bin. Ned had opened it. It was in this way, she supposed, that traces of the dead removed themselves from everyday life. All that would be left would be his works on the shelf: books about Ibsen. Then no doubt his view of Ibsen would finally fall out of fashion. The books would drift off to the second-hand bookstalls, and on to a few, idiosyncratic, old-codgery shelves; and just a handful of people would be left to say, wonderingly, 'Ned Ludd – that rings a bell,' and the bell would be for Ned Ludd, the Leicestershire village idiot, who in 1782 destroyed a stocking frame on the grounds that it was putting him out of a job, and after whom the Luddite rioters were named. Not Ned Ludd, the Ibsen scholar. Not even Alexandra Ludd, actress, who once used to get her name and her picture in the paper so often: Nora in *A Doll's House*, at a time when women had decided to make Nora their mascot in their final drive to be free of male tyranny. Perhaps there'd be some reference to the Ludds for scholars, in the theatrical section of some CD Rom. There'd be so little left for people to do in the future-present, they'd have nothing better to do than put up the past on the screen, and stare at it;

listen to the voice saying: 'Ludd, Ned', and reading out the supporting text. No one would bother to read. Why make the effort?

Jenny Linden. Why had Diamond gone off with her so readily? It was out of character. Diamond was suspicious of most people, unless he knew them well. The house seemed eerily quiet: now that the dog's broken breathing, wheezes and snorts were not there, she noticed them. Alexandra suddenly missed Sascha: the sudden determined rushings of his little feet, the energy in the air that meant he was about. It was too early to call Irene. But Sascha would be up: he would be in front of the television, staring at the Teletext he couldn't read. It was, he averred, his favourite programme. He must come home as soon as possible. She wanted her arms around him.

She poured the coffee but did not drink it.

Jenny Linden. Jenny Linden never got asked to the Ludd parties. Why not? Others yet more foolish, yet more hopeless, got asked along. Jenny used her little podgy fingers and her enthusiasm to earn her living. She was the theatrical equivalent of an architectural model maker. She would sew, in miniature, the costumes the designer had in his or her head so that the director could approve, alter, enthuse or carp. It was a perfectly respectable occupation. It brought her in a living wage. She lived in a little period cottage in Eddon Gurney, opposite the prison. Ned had once taken her, Alexandra, to visit Jenny in her studio, which turned out to be her front room. He wanted Alexandra to see the costumes Jenny was doing for a production of *Peer Gynt* – an exact copy of those used for the London production of 1911. The visit must have been four years ago: she remembered being pregnant with Sascha at the time. Ned had rung Jenny in advance, to say they were coming. It had been a perfectly formal visit. Jenny had opened a bottle of wine, fluttered her pleasure at a visit which evidently meant a lot to her, and showed off the little dolls' dresses with, to Alexandra, pathetic pride. Ned had asked if he could photograph them for his book on *Peer Gynt*

33

and Jenny had said yes. What had happened since to give Jenny cause to say she loved Ned, Alexandra had no idea.

Except of course Jenny was the sort of person who loves everything and everyone at the same level. She would 'love' her therapist, 'love' her friends, 'love' Ned because he had once taken some notice of her. Why would Jenny think she, Alexandra, didn't love Ned? *Erratum:* hadn't loved Ned. Because Alexandra hadn't been there when Ned died? Jenny was probably the kind of woman who'd cling like a limpet just in case someone died and they weren't there, and that way hasten their death.

She remembered Jenny saying, though she couldn't remember where, or when, or in what company,
'I have this wonderful therapist. She gave me the courage to leave my husband,' and thinking, 'Lonely women are always saying that.'

Somewhere there had been a husband and a son, both rejected in the interests of Jenny's talent. The husband a lighting director in the West End; yes, that was it. A technician, not an artist. Not even a critic. Jenny was the kind who longed aggressively for the peace of the countryside, to live next to nature; to discover her true self, that kind of stuff. Ned was in the country because there was somewhere to park and he could have a rest from theatrical folk.

Why was she even giving Jenny Linden two minutes' thought? A mad woman, excited by death, roaming the edge of the territory. She wasn't worth it. Alexandra had seen herself as duty bound to ask her round, from time to time – a neighbour in vaguely the same profession – and Ned would say, 'For God's sake, not Jenny Linden. She'll bore everyone to death, and talk about animal rights.'

Alexandra wondered by what right she and Ned had felt it their entitlement to dole out social acceptability or otherwise round the neighbourhood. If the Ludds said people were OK, they were. Now Ned had gone, had toppled in death through the linking of a protective fence of their own devising – the one that kept the boring and pitiable out – and broken it, now heaven knew who'd come rushing in. And it might even serve Alexandra right.

Alexandra went to the living room and under the gaze of Leda entwined with her swan, and Europa petting her bull – both deities in porcelain, *circa* 1760, and a Dog of Fo, in salt-glazed stoneware, around 1730 – took down Ned's book on *Peer Gynt*. The book fell open on a photograph of Jenny Linden's little set, little figures, tiny dresses. The caption read: 'Photo: Ned Ludd. Jenny Linden's brilliant and exquisite re-creation of the 1922 production at the Old Vic.'

You could either assume Ned had gone back at some other time to take pictures of Jenny's work on the 1922 production, or that the caption was wrong, or that Ned had been in error in the first place. Or that she, Alexandra, had misremembered 1911.

Alexandra heard a movement behind her and whirled, and there was Jenny Linden staring at her. In her, Alexandra's, living room. 'I brought Diamond back,' said Jenny Linden. 'I came straight in. I hope you don't mind.'
'I do, actually,' said Alexandra.
'I did so hope we could be friends,' said Jenny. 'We both need someone to talk to.'
'A trouble shared is a trouble halved, that kind of thing?' enquired Alexandra.
'Don't mock,' said Jenny Linden. 'You're very clever and smart, but it doesn't help in the end. I know that book by heart. *Peer Gynt and the Nordic Imagination.* Ned was such a wise and wonderful man. I don't suppose you even read it. Ned said you were never interested in his work.'
'Just get out of my house,' said Alexandra, but Jenny stayed where she was, with a kind of stolid, stubborn lumpenness, as if she hadn't heard what Alexandra said, or perhaps Alexandra had only thought it, not spoken it.

'You're upset,' said Jenny. 'I'll make you a cup of tea.'

Alexandra followed Jenny into the kitchen. Jenny was taking mugs from the cupboard, the teapot from the shelf, without hesitation, as if this were her own home. Diamond lay under the table, exhausted and panting, thumping his tail from time to time, and looking strangely guilty.

Alexandra advanced on Jenny and slapped her across the cheek. Jenny dropped a mug and stared, stupefied.
'You're violent,' she said. 'On top of everything. You really do need treatment. Ned was right.'

But still she didn't go. She moved her little hands up to her pink cheek. Jenny Linden had a squidged-up face, as if the chin aimed up for the eyebrows, the ears longed to get to the nose. She had a puffy little bosom and a thick waist. Ned would not have looked at her twice. This woman was in some fantasy of her own. In twelve years Ned had only once disconcerted Alexandra, by yearning after Glenn Close, whom he admired for her intelligence and temperament as much as her looks.
'You're just back here to lay your greedy hands on what you can,' spat Jenny Linden. 'You don't care about Ned. It breaks my heart.'
Alexandra kicked Jenny Linden's shins hard. Jenny Linden hopped about and finally ran out of the kitchen door. Alexandra slammed it after her and locked it. Alexandra went to the phone and called Abbie.
'Jenny Linden's been here,' said Alexandra. 'Is she mad or what?'
'Oh dear,' said Abbie. 'I'd better come over.'
'Tell me now, on the phone,' said Alexandra. But Abbie only repeated that she'd come over as soon as she could, with Arthur.

Alexandra inspected her house for traces of Jenny Linden, or others. She looked in the bathroom mirror, and for a second thought she saw Jenny Linden looking back at her, but it was

36

just a trick of the light. She felt disloyal to Ned for checking up on him; like this, after his death.

'You're too bad, Ned,' she said. 'Whatever did you say to that dreadful deluded creature? There must have been something.' But there was no reply from Ned. It wasn't that she expected words – how could she? – rather a momentary joining, a fleeting acknowledgement, some brief touching of his spirit with hers. A laugh that ought to be shared: a dismissal of doubt; a dismissal of Jenny Linden. 'Dire Jenny Linden, gone completely round the twist!' Ned would have said, could have said.

Alexandra looked through cupboards, drawers, the kitchen shelves, the bathroom cabinet. She no longer knew what she was looking for. Everywhere familiar things, some worthless, some priceless, everything redolent of a present which had so un-expectedly turned into a past. Everywhere was Ned. She would have to remove so much – pack stuff up, burn some things, give others away, in order to reclaim the present for herself, forget the future.

Abbie had cleaned up before she, Alexandra, arrived: she'd emptied ashtrays, run the dishwasher through, even changed the sheets. Why? Abbie's nervous mind, she supposed. And where was Ned's toothbrush? Missing. Hers was there, and Sascha's, but not Ned's. The tooth mug needed cleaning: tooth mugs always did.

She went into the bedroom and looked through Ned's sock drawer and for the first time wept without worrying about her eyes. She even knuckled them and howled. Then she found a red suspender belt with black lace trimmings among the socks. Her own, she supposed. Except she couldn't remember ever owning such a thing. Perhaps before she was married? She tried it on over her jeans. It was too big for her. Even so, she couldn't fasten it behind her back: she had to tug the clasp round to the front to do it. A kind of trick fastening: you slipped one bit of plastic into another at an angle, then flattened it and it snapped to. Except she couldn't do it, even looking at it. She gave up and let the belt just fall to the floor. Wouldn't you know how to fasten your own suspender belt? Not if it was years old, pre-marriage, pre-motherhood, in the stockings-and-suspender party days. You'd have forgotten. She supposed.

She looked under the bed: nothing: spick and span. There were the usual two suitcases there. They'd been dusted. Theresa the help had been away for the week in Spain. Theresa was seventeen and as many stone. Theresa had trouble vacuuming under the beds: she didn't bend easily in her middle. Abbie must have done it. The carpet was a little damp, towards the window. Had it rained? Alexandra couldn't remember. When the rain was from the west, fine and strong, water could creep into the room between window frame and window, forcing itself in along with the delicate new tendrils of Virginia creeper. Perhaps that was it. But when she'd been weeding the pansies the soil had been dry, dry, dry.

Alexandra had a sudden clear impression that Ned had died on the bed, not downstairs at all. That for some reason nobody had told her this. But that was absurd. Why would they lie? Perhaps they'd thought it would make her reluctant to sleep in her own bed? They were wrong. She wanted to be where Ned's last breaths had been. Perhaps such breaths lingered in the air and she detected them. She lay down upon the coverlet and fell asleep. Diamond crept up the stairs and lay beside her.

The phone woke her. She went downstairs to answer it. There was no extension in the bedroom. It was the *Daily Mail* asking her how she felt. She put the phone down. It rang again. The caller was the assistant to a broadsheet's theatre critic, saying she was sorry to disturb Alexandra at a time like this, but could the paper have advance notice of the funeral: they would be sending a photographer: such a great loss. Alexandra put the phone down.

The doorbell went. A flashbulb popped in her face. She slammed the door shut, went into the kitchen, grabbed a knife, and crouched the other side of the door. The bell rang again. She opened the door quickly, brandishing the knife. But it was only a bunch of flowers from the local florist, cellophane-wrapped. They were from Jenny Linden.

'Forgive and forget,' it read. 'In fond friendship, Jenny.'

Alexandra threw them after the florist, and then, as they scattered over the path, noticed a man with a camera standing among the long artichokes, beneath the clothes line, where the green sheets from the marital bed had lately hung to dry. 'Just a minute there!' he called to her, so she quickly went inside and called the police. They said they'd send someone as soon as possible.

The phone rang. It was Abbie. She said she couldn't get over because one of her Japanese students had choked on a plum stone and become hysterical. No, the girl was fine physically, just humiliated. The Japanese were like that. Abbie would come over in the afternoon. She'd hoped Jenny Linden would stay quiet and out of the way, but apparently not. The only thing to do with her was physically to throw her out.

'That's what I did,' said Alexandra.

'She's had a crush on Ned for years,' said Abbie. 'She's on the verge of psychopathic. She'd hang round in the garden a lot. He's had to call the police. You know, like *Fatal Attraction* but without the sex. A total fan. A kind of sub-stalker.'

'Why didn't Ned tell me?'

'It was embarrassing, I suppose,' said Abbie.

'Why didn't *you* tell me?' asked Alexandra.

'She was so pathetic. It was so ridiculous. I just thought she'd go away or be locked up or something, and we'd all forget it. I'd rather tell you this in person. It's so cold like this. Can't it wait till this afternoon?'

'No. It's Wednesday. Hamish is coming this afternoon.'

'Thank God for that. At least you'll have someone there to keep you company.'

'You called me at five-thirty on Sunday morning,' said Alexandra. 'I was there by Sunday lunchtime. In that time you called the police, the doctor, me, Vilna, and the ambulance, and you cleaned my house from top to bottom, and washed my sheets.'

'I didn't do any cleaning,' said Abbie. 'I just changed the sheets and ran the old ones through the washing machine. If you run a residential language school it gets to be second nature. If in doubt change the sheets and serve food. Joke?'

Alexandra laughed a little.

'That's better,' said Abbie.

'Then who did the cleaning?' asked Alexandra. 'Theresa's still away. It wasn't her.'

'I expect Ned did. He's not hopeless. You hadn't been home since the previous Tuesday.'

'He doesn't vacuum under beds if it means moving two suitcases. Sorry, delete doesn't. Insert was not accustomed to.'

'Vilna might have done it,' said Abbie, ignoring Alexandra's joke. 'During the morning Vilna may have run round with the vacuum and the duster. People behave oddly when there's a body in the house.'

'Abbie, that's my body,' said Alexandra, and began to choke and cry. 'And this is my house. I don't want strangers like Vilna and Jenny Linden making free with it.'

'Oh God,' said Abbie. 'I ought to be with you. I'm coming over. The Japanese girl will just have to do without me.' She put the phone down.

Alexandra went to the door and looked round. The photographer had gone; there was no sign of Jenny Linden. Flowers dozed in the sun. There was the gentlest of breezes. There were broad beans on the tall pole pyramids which needed picking. She'd try and do it this evening. Ned fretted if the pods stayed on the plants long enough to become stringy. She lived in a beautiful house, in a beautiful place. She was a widow.

She called the Eddon Gurney police station to say not to bother to send anyone up; everything was now quiet. They were relieved because they were understaffed; they'd take it off their list of calls; they expressed their sorrow about her husband's death. Ned Ludd was such a loss to the community. Would she be staying in the house?

'Of course,' she said.

They'd thought she might be selling, moving up to London altogether, to the bright lights. Wouldn't have much time for slow country folk and their country ways. What was to keep her in the countryside now?

Alexandra resisted the temptation to say if they talked less they might have got someone over earlier to chase the photographer out of her garden, but it is never wise to rile the police so she said, with truth, how much she loved the area, how after twelve years The Cottage felt like home; now that her husband had died she would need more than ever the support of the community, and so forth, and they said call if there was any trouble and they'd be up at once. To let them know.

Abbie called Alexandra to say she couldn't come over. Now a young Gulf Arab boy had bitten into a plum and got stung on the tongue by a wasp, and though there seemed no swelling they'd thought it best to call the doctor.

Alexandra suggested that Arthur cut down the plum tree.

'Abbie,' she asked. 'There are still some things you haven't told me. Jenny Linden was in the house on Sunday morning. Did she just turn up, or what? Or did you call her too?'

'Of course I didn't call her. She was outside the house when I arrived,' said Abbie. 'In the front, behind the privet hedge. Kind of lurking. Ned once told me she'd do that, in the very early mornings. Sometimes when he let Diamond out first thing Jenny Linden would be there, and she and Diamond would go off for a walk together. Well, it saved Ned walking the dog himself, didn't it?'

'You mean Ned used her? She was obsessed with him and he used her? To walk Diamond?'

'It's not so bad a thing, Alexandra,' said Abbie mildly. 'When you think of other male sins. He felt bad about Jenny. Her life was so empty, he said. He tried all kinds of things to make her leave him alone. Being horrid, being nice, appealing to reason.

41

Perhaps he thought if Diamond wore her out she'd give up. Diamond would wear anyone out.'

'How long has it been going on?'

'A couple of years, I suppose.'

'Years?' Alexandra was incredulous. 'Who knew about this?'

'Most people, I suppose.'

Alexandra absorbed this.

'Extraordinary,' she said.

'Not really,' said Abbie. 'If someone's having an affair the partner's always the last to know. No one likes to be the one to break the news; and anyway they think it will all go away, or even perhaps they're wrong. Of course this wasn't an affair, don't think that. Jenny just pestered him. She's an obsessive.'

'But people like that can be dangerous,' said Alexandra. 'Sometimes they even kill. I should have been told.'

'You're an artist,' said Abbie, with just a hint of malice. 'No one wants to upset you. You have to be away from home a lot; you can't help it: not much fun for you to know there's a mad woman stalking your husband.'

'It's not a bundle of laughs,' said Alexandra. 'Then what happened?'

'I opened the back door, Diamond ran out and went off with Jenny,' said Abbie. 'Then I looked through the window and saw the body and came in and started making phone calls, then Jenny came back with Diamond, right into the house, and saw the body and had hysterics and ran round like a mad thing all morning tearing her hair as if she were in some Greek tragedy. So I called Vilna because she's good at seeing people off, and Vilna did; she saw Jenny Linden off. Vilna can be marvellous.'

'Well, whatever Vilna did then,' said Alexandra, 'Jenny Linden's come back. She's unbalanced. One moment she wants to be friends, the next she hates me.'

'That's what Ned said,' observed Abbie. 'She's unbalanced. That always seemed to be the worst sin in Ned's eyes. He didn't like nutty people. The only reason he liked me was because I was so observably sane, I sometimes think. Alexandra, I have to go. The doctor's coming up the drive.'

'Dr Moebius?'

42

'Yes.'

'Isn't he in his surgery?'

'Wasp stings to the tongue count as an emergency, especially if it's an Arab princeling with enough money to buy up all Eddon Gurney.'

Abbie went to answer the door to the doctor. The student with the stung tongue met her in the corridor and said, carefully, 'I might have just imagined it, having seen the wasp fly away.' He got his tenses right and Arthur, who had also gone to answer the door, was pleased with him; Abbie less so. It was the school's responsibility to pay for medical emergencies, and Dr Moebius had been called out, and would charge. Dr Moebius went away, but gave the lad an injection, just to be on the safe side. Anti histamine.

Alexandra left the house and drove the half-mile to Vilna's place. Vilna lived in a small mansion in a charming, olde-world village where property prices were the highest around. The house was called Pineapple Lodge because of two large carved stone pine-apples, *circa* 1750, sitting on each of the gateposts which flanked the wrought-iron gates (Coalbrookdale, 1830) to the drive. The gate, once permanently open, was now permanently closed, and could be opened only by remote control from inside the house. Security devices were everywhere. Vilna's husband was in prison. He was an Australian junk-bond dealer who had run into trouble with the law three years back. Most of his properties had been sold, except for this one, originally purchased for Vilna's mother, who had got out of Yugoslavia just before the country collapsed into little murderous parts, and could enter five songs, not one, for the Eurovision Song Contest. Here the two women, mother and daughter, waited until the time came when Clive would be paroled. Then their plan was to move to South Africa. In the meantime they made do with the West Country. Clive had many enemies, and they felt safer here. Strange faces in a remote country area were quickly spotted and obliged to account for themselves.

Ned and Alexandra had been to visit Vilna once or twice, but had been taken aback by the style and colour of the soft furnishings in a house rigorous in its original simplicity.

'It shouldn't matter,' said Ned, 'that the place looks like a Turkish harem, but it does. It makes it hard to take Vilna seriously.' The English countryside, everyone knew, was a place where mud must be taken into account, and dogs, and bicycles: where the furniture was oak or pine, antique, and where wealth was always understated. Ned said this was the Englishman's traditional defence against the mob. Only the rich and knowledgeable could tell wealth from poverty. Even Mrs Edwards, the live-in housekeeper, would complain at the store that her employers simply didn't know how to behave. They were ostentatious and didn't fit in.

The Cottage went for the most part unlocked – who could tell that that scrawl on the battered wall was a Picasso; that the old wood box was a Jacobean coffer, the coal scuttle a fine piece of Arts and Crafts in beaten copper; that the blackened fireback, *circa* 1705, was priceless? Vilna and Maria's house, with its elaborately papered walls, its swathes of curtains, its plump sofas, its mahogany and walnut furniture, the plenitude of ormolu, and with TV and video everywhere in sight, was obviously worth robbing. Not just a casual village break-in, either. The real, planned stuff. What one villain owed to another. Clive Mansell's family home.

So Vilna, not fitting in, was kept on the outskirts of the social life which centred round The Cottage and which easily embraced most of the eccentrics in the area – not quite excluded, not quite included. She would be asked to lunch, but seldom to dinner. That her husband was in prison was not held against her – he was a financial wizard, not any kind of common criminal, and had probably been framed anyway. So Abbie, who liked Vilna, and rather cared for vulgar cocktails clinking with ice served in elaborate glasses by the side of the swimming pool, told everyone, and many believed her.

44

Alexandra knew well enough that she herself was not exempt from local criticism. All right for Ned, although a newcomer to the area, to be a writer and critic. The occupation was familiar. There'd always been those about, moved down from the city: Thomas Hardy being an earlier example. Just about all right for Alexandra to be an actress, so long as she was a failed actress, a woman trying to get pregnant – for as such they defined her, once the receptionist at the surgery had spread the news. Alexandra was acceptable inasmuch as her husband was, and as long as she was unfortunate and could be pitied. But once her fortunes changed, once the run of *A Doll's House* had started, once her picture was in the paper, once she'd had her photograph taken with Princess Anne – and since she now had a child and couldn't be pitied and, worse, had more or less handed the child over to be looked after by Theresa the help – she was seen as flashy. Sussex would be a better county for her.

'Vilna,' said Alexandra, 'what do you know about Jenny Linden?'
'I try not to think about her,' said Vilna. 'Why depress oneself? She is quite mad. Why don't you forget her?'
'Because she makes it difficult,' said Alexandra. 'She keeps popping up. And because I have no idea what there is to forget. No one says anything clearly enough. If Jenny Linden was going round pestering my husband, why didn't you tell me?'
'Darling, I don't know you very well. We have been acquaintances, not friends. That has not been my doing. People round here are stand-offish. Abbie told me that word. Abbie is your friend: she should have told you. But she was too English. She thought if she looked the other way it would go away. She told me that.'
'I am sorry if I have seemed stand-offish,' said Alexandra, and she was. In the grim light of death anyone who lives seems valuable. Though the light quickly fades and we are back to normal. 'I have just been so busy lately.
'Did Ned encourage Jenny Linden in any way?' she asked. 'Had he given her any reason to behave in the way she is?'
'You know Ned, darling,' said Vilna. 'Always the ladies' man.'
'No, I didn't know him as that way at all,' said Alexandra stiffly,

45

deciding she preferred Vilna as an acquaintance not a friend after all. 'Ned was a very wife-and-child sort of man. A family man.'

'One can be so wrong about people,' said Vilna. 'Even if married to them. I lived with Clive for four years and never knew he was a crim. I learnt that word from his friends. It is short for criminal.'

Vilna and Alexandra sat at the bar of the swimming pool and had drinks. Plum trees bent over the glass roof as if trying to get at the water below. The swimming pool, Alexandra realised, was where once the walled kitchen garden had been. The end wall of the room still incorporated some original Elizabethan brick. Everywhere else was gold and black mosaic.

'Isn't this a fantastic pool? Otto Cavalier was the interior designer, darling, did you know?'

Alexandra said she'd never heard of Otto Cavalier, which didn't go down too well. She returned to the subject of Clive, in which she felt safe.

'Nobody around here believes Clive is a criminal,' said Alexandra politely. 'Not even his city colleagues. He was framed; he was a sacrificial victim. Everyone knows that. You mustn't feel bad about it.'

'He is a crim,' said Vilna firmly. 'I know that for a fact. An English judge said so and British law is the envy of the world. That is one of the reasons my mother and I came to this country in the first place. Your husband was not a criminal but he was certainly highly sexed. He would press any pretty woman up against a wall at a party; at least that was my experience. You would not want it otherwise, I suppose? Who wants a gelded horse when they can have the real thing?'

Alexandra, who had never thought of Vilna as pretty, just rather over made-up, decided Vilna was one of those women who are convinced that all men have designs upon them, so deluded are they about their own attractions. She did not have the energy to defend Ned's reputation. She simply discounted Vilna's account of him.

'Tell me about Sunday morning,' she said.

46

'Abbie called me at about ten in the morning and I went round to The Cottage,' said Vilna, as if she had been rehearsed. 'When I got there the ambulance was just leaving with the body. I was disappointed. I'd never seen a dead body.'

'I'm so sorry you were disappointed,' said Alexandra.

'Darling, I have offended you!' cried Vilna. 'I am so tactless. Cancel, cancel, as they say! There was Jenny Linden running up and down like a cat in a seizure with hardly a stitch of clothing on. I could afford to run around like that; believe me, Jenny Linden cannot. Flop, bounce, wobble! I would be so ashamed. That woman could afford to lose at least thirty pounds.'

'No clothes on?'

'She had one of your nighties on. I think Abbie made her put it on, to save her modesty. But it was very light and lacey. Dr Moebius gave her pills but they made no difference at all.'

'Dr Moebius gave Jenny Linden pills?'

'It might have been a jab, darling, I don't know. I wasn't there. Forget it, darling. Your husband is gone. All men are bastards. Find another one, better than the last.'

'I need to get things clear in my head,' said Alexandra. 'I know you are all trying to protect me but I wish you wouldn't. And my husband was not all men, he was not a bastard. I love him.'

'It is only a figure of speech,' said Vilna. 'Customary in this country.'

'How exactly did you see Jenny Linden off?' enquired Alexandra.

'I hit her,' said Vilna. 'Forget it. We're on your side, Alexandra.'

'There isn't a side to be on,' said Alexandra. 'Jenny Linden is just a sodding nuisance. I don't want her saying anything to the fucking newspapers. What has Ned dying got to do with her? I don't want her coming to the funeral, the bitch!'

'There is no need to swear,' said the wild woman of the mountain tribes, primly.

'So why did you feel obliged to vacuum my house?' enquired Alexandra.

'Because at home whenever I am in a crisis, I clean,' said Vilna, 'like many women, and because it needed it, and because I am your friend, and you were coming home to more than enough.'

'Yes, I was,' said Alexandra. 'I did. Thank you.'

The two women smiled at one another. Alexandra drank her cocktail with a straw bent in the middle, designed to bypass chunks of pineapple, little flags and maraschino cherries. It was absurd.

'Where did Abbie find my lace nightie?' asked Alexandra.

'Darling, you are so suspicious. You must not let yourself become paranoic. I have no idea. Your cupboard, your drawer?'

'Under my pillow, I expect. Why did she have to do that? It moves Jenny Linden far too close to Ned. It makes me feel ill.'

'It was just something loose Abbie could throw over Jenny. Like a cloth you throw over a birdcage to keep its occupant quiet.'

'I came to thank you both for helping me out. I'm not quite myself at the moment.'

'You're welcome,' said Vilna.

'When you saw the body in the morgue,' said Alexandra, 'what did Ned look like? I've never seen a dead body either. Is it frightening?'

'He didn't look very dead to me. He looked astonished. Death tautens the jaw, like a facelift. It is very flattering. I was sorry, seeing him lying there, I hadn't said yes. It's a criminal waste of opportunity, don't you think, saying no? We're on this earth for such a little time; we're cold and dark for so long.'

'Say no to what? I don't understand you.'

'He said he kept the door unlocked when you were away so beautiful women could visit him at night. It was an invitation.'

'Vilna, it was a joke. Ned talks like that.'

'He was not my type anyway. And he was married to you. And you are my friend. And the dog would have jumped up. You English and your dogs.'

'It saves security gates,' said Alexandra, 'in the middle of the countryside.'

'Your husband looks very peaceful in death and younger than in life. Jenny Linden looked at his corpse and screamed.'

'Jenny Linden saw the body? How do you know?'

'As Abbie and I left the morgue, Jenny Linden was coming in. We nearly crashed into her. Abbie's a bad, bad driver. We had to stop. The other car went on. While Abbie was inspecting the damage I heard Jenny Linden scream.'

'Everyone's been to see the body except for me? Even Jenny Linden?'

'Alexandra,' said Vilna, 'you didn't want to come with us. That was seen as strange.'

'I was exhausted,' said Alexandra. 'I was in suspension. You should have waited until I'd been. I can't see any point in seeing the corpse, it's been so picked over. I'd rather remember him alive.'

'Ned said you would often be very tired. Career women so often are. It is the penalty men pay in return for their wives' salaries. I have never worked in all my life. I wouldn't dream of it.'

She clicked her fingers and her mother appeared from nowhere with more drinks. She was wearing pink rubber sandals with very thick stockings. She went away again. Vilna did not speak to her.

'How does Jenny Linden get to The Cottage? Does she drive or does she walk?' asked Alexandra, choosing to ignore this last. 'Or perhaps she comes on a broomstick.'

'She didn't have her car on Sunday. After I'd hit her and she'd stopped running round and screaming, I had to drive her back. She wouldn't have been fit to drive anyway. She clung to the doorhandle; she kept saying it was her house by rights, I had to drag her away. She complained no one was being nice to her. I said you were on your way, in all decency she had to stay away, and I offered her £200 to make sure she did. I thought that was about the right sum. Not too little, not too much. A tip.'

'You what?'

'Money's nothing,' said Vilna. 'I felt for you. Women like Jenny Linden can be dangerous. At home where people are sensible they are found dead in a ditch; knifed. Here you do not use knives, you use money. My mother and I follow the customs of the country. It is advisable. Do you want to see my new crown?' she asked. She opened her mouth and Alexandra looked inside.

'Very nice,' she said, and went to visit Jenny Linden.

7

Jenny Linden's house was in the old part of town: a row of cottages facing a wide but secluded street, on the other side of it being the high brick wall of Eddon Gurney prison, built 1718, and now Grade One Listed as a building of prime architectural and heritage interest. The prison had been recently taken out of service: the level of absenteeism and suicide amongst its staff had finally impinged upon the authorities; no amount of reorganisation or counselling, it seemed, could ameliorate the terror and fear that oozed out of the old stone walls. But the city council had begun the work of converting the building into a Penitentiary Theme Park, the first of its kind in the land.

Number 42 sat snugly among its similar neighbours: two-storey cottages with thick walls, built to house the prison warders. A plaster front, a porched front door, a large square window to the right, a kitchen out the back, two bedrooms, and a bathroom extension above the kitchen. Out the back door was a little square garden. Once such a dwelling would have housed a man, a wife, an aunt or so and some children. Now it served very well as a love nest for one. Cosy.

There was a parking space outside, but Alexandra left her car a little way down the road. She looked through Jenny Linden's window but saw no one inside. A rather handsome orange cat sat on the inside sill, next to a well-cared-for pot plant, and stared bleakly at her. Alexandra could see beyond cat and plant into a room which was vaguely arty: orange throws over ethnic wicker chairs, a large table on which were the bits and pieces of work in progress – bits of card, pieces of fabric – an easel; a rug on a polished floor; theatre posters on the walls; photographs everywhere. She could not make out the detail. A zodiac lamp; a deep sofa on which a couple could copulate, just about.

Alexandra rang the front doorbell. No one came. She looked up and down the road. No one. Children were at school, adults at work. These were aspiring little houses; not for those on welfare. Alexandra slipped a credit card between lock and hasp and pushed. It was how she opened the door of her London flat, after the show, after the late-night supper, if she had forgotten her key. Jenny Linden's door opened. Such a method of entry would never have worked at Vilna's house. Alexandra went inside. The house smelt of lavender toilet water and scented soap, of paint and glue. There was a sense of desperation in the air, of serenity suddenly shattered: a coat which should have been on a peg fallen on the floor and not picked up; in the small kitchen a bag of shopping left on the floor and still unpacked. Frozen food losing its hardness, going soggy: the opposite of a dead body, which started soggy and went hard. The silence felt temporary, as if recently rent by tears and wails which would at any moment start again.

Alexandra went to the front window, pulled the curtains; switched on the lamp. On the table, open, was a diary. There were few entries: crosses here and there, and question marks. Today's entry: 'Bristol, 12–1, Leah.' Bristol was twenty miles away. It was now five past twelve. Jenny Linden had dropped everything to get to her therapist. She had not taken her address book with her. That was open by the telephone. Alexandra's address book was crammed and messy. Jenny's was neat, but there were few entries. Ned's name wasn't there, not under L, not under N. Alexandra herself was there, in the A's. Her London address and telephone number. How had Jenny Linden come by that?

Alexandra looked at the photographs pinned up on the wall. Ned everywhere. Ned at parties at The Cottage, Ned with Diamond in the garden, Ned in the garden putting up the beanstalk pyramids. He did that every year. Who had taken these? Jenny?

51

Lurked behind the hedge and snapped away? Had she stolen them, acquired them from Ned himself? Or entered The Cottage when they were both away and pried into the family photographs? It was horrible to think of that. They locked the house only if it was empty, but anyone who knew the house could break in easily enough. And Jenny Linden seemed to know the house so well. She couldn't talk to Ned about it. She would never be able to ask Ned anything again. The photographs had a curious flatness, as photographs do when they represent the dead, not the living. 'The dead' was a strange notion: you could define it only by a negative: someone, something, once alive, now not. A rock wasn't 'dead' – it was just inanimate. Alexandra found she was standing in the centre of Jenny Linden's living room, in suspension once again, thoughts looping. Whatever her business was here, and she was not yet quite sure what it was, she could not afford to waste time. She did not want to be discovered by Jenny Linden. The orange cat stared at her; slowly got to its four feet, arched its back idly, and walked from the room to sit by the front door. She worried for a moment in case it could talk, but that was absurd. A thought transposed from her thoughts about Diamond. If he could talk, what would he say? It seemed wilful of him not to, as if he wasn't on her side. But this wasn't a matter of 'sides'. Why did she feel under attack? Well, obviously – mad Jenny Linden. Enough to unsettle anyone, make them worry in case cats talked.

Ned's books on the shelves; a letter in Ned's handwriting on the board above the table. Dated two years ago. 'Dear Jenny – thanks for the *Rosmersholm* pics. Brilliant as usual. Talk to you soon. In haste, Ned.' And two crosses for kisses beneath the familiar signature. Well, what was wrong with that? Ned always put two crosses for kisses, for friends. Or was it one? She herself got three. Jesus, was she in competition here?

On the table was a cheque for £200 signed 'Vilna Mansell'. It lay there as if no attention had been paid to it at all. It was dated last Sunday. Well, someone sometimes told the truth. Vilna too was barking mad, but at least had the excuse of war back home, and saw herself as Alexandra's friend, to the value of a couple of hundred pounds. She was troubled.

Alexandra stared at the photographs some more. She thought she herself had taken the one of Ned putting up the bean poles. That had been in May. Three months ago. She'd taken the roll to Boots the chemist to be developed. Most people did the same. If Jenny had an arrangement with someone at Boots she could siphon off any number of photos of Ned. Just ask her to look out for them; have another copy made. Alexandra observed that Jenny had burned away her half of a snapshot of the two of them, herself and Ned down at Kimmeridge Bay, where the fossils lurked in the flaky slate cliffs. Abbie had taken that. They'd all gone down in the car. Three years ago. Had they met Jenny Linden and her husband there, accidentally? Shared the contents of the Lindens' thermos of coffee? She seemed to have some such memory. Dave Linden, that was his name. Had Sascha been in that snapshot too? Alexandra thought so. The burn marks ran up the side of Ned's sleeve.

All I have here, thought Alexandra, is evidence of a woman obsessed by my husband. A plain, mad, unhappy woman. I should feel sorry for her.

Alexandra went upstairs to Jenny Linden's tiny bedroom. A white coverlet on the unmade bed; lots of cushions and pillows tossed everywhere, black lace knickers on the floor, trimmed with crimson. Black and crimson – well, she'd worn that too in her time. Vulgar and fun. Just odd for Jenny Linden. But perhaps she lived in hope. Women did. A fossilised ammonite on the wooden mantelpiece. You could find them in the ground round here. They were excavating part of the prison to build their Penitentiary Theme Park. All kinds of things turned up in the disturbed soil. Roman pottery. Stone Age axeheads. Fossils. Presumably once sea had covered the land here; presumably Jenny Linden kept her eyes open. Finding fossils was the kind of thing that Ned approved of.

Still the quiver in the air as if the wails had just stopped. A painting of Ned on the wall: no, not a painting. A kind of montage of scraps of fabric which amounted to a portrait; very much Jenny's style. A model of a set on the dressing table: on closer inspection a model of Ned and Alexandra's bedroom. That was shocking. The oak table made in matches; the brass bed contrived in orange sticks and minute slivers of twisted gold paper. A doll's house mirror where her, Alexandra's, mirror was. How did Jenny know what her bedroom looked like? Because she'd been to a party at The Cottage in the past? Might even have come to an event or so when Alexandra had been in town? Ned sometimes asked people round? If the spare room was occupied, guests would leave their coats in the master bedroom. Or because when Ned and Alexandra were both away Jenny Linden came in and loitered, and breathed up her beloved's breath? A fan, a true fan, a devotee, a groupie, a stupid, plain, fat middle-aged woman well beyond her sell-by date, a stalker into sympathetic magic.

Alexandra went into the bathroom and found Ned's toothbrush in the tooth mug. That is to say it was yellow and had a blue line running through the tufts. When the blue line was no longer visible it was time to buy a new toothbrush. It was barely visible. Perhaps Abbie had thrown it out on the Sunday morning? Perhaps Jenny had then stolen it? Perhaps she welcomed this dreadful intimacy – that she should put in her own mouth what had been in Ned's?

Alexandra took the toothbrush. She took all the photographs of Ned off the wall. She took the address book and the diary. She let the orange cat out, who stalked away calmly up the road. And she drove home to the unbearable emptiness of The Cottage. She would not have to put up with it for long. Hamish would be arriving mid-afternoon.

There were eight messages on the answerphone. One from the *Mail on Sunday*, another from *The Times* asking for help with Ned's obituary, another from Dr Moebius asking her to return his latest call, one weeping woman too incoherent to identify, one from the florist asking her where exactly The Cottage was, and another one, which Ned had picked up: Ned saying, 'Is that you, Leah? Hang on a minute, I'll switch off the bloody answerphone.' At least she thought he said that. She replayed it. It was an old call. The tape was on its second time around. Trying to find it again, she erased the message by accident. But she thought he'd said that. Perhaps he'd said 'dear'? Soon she would be as mad as Jenny Linden.

Alexandra felt completely excluded, cut out, burned away. Ned's image was owned by others, as was his voice: it spoke to others, not to her. Even his body, his skull, had been snatched by others. Were they sawing through it at this moment? Did bones leave sawdust behind? Did brains spill out as they did in horror stories? Diamond snuffled round her ankles. She made a fire in the grate. She burned the photographs because Ned's image had been besmirched by Jenny's regard. She burned the toothbrush because it might have been in Jenny's mouth and had become disgusting. She lay it on a firelighter, applied a match, and watched it splutter and flare. She watched Ned disappearing in green and purple and black. But he still didn't feel gone. If she turned round he'd be smiling at her. Like the smile of the Cheshire Cat, remaining long after the body had gone.

If Jenny had been less sludge-like, had been a prettier, younger, cleverer person, Alexandra would not feel so shop-soiled, so picked over. Jenny was like a garment in a jumble sale: infinitely dreary. Grief should be pure and noble.

There were noises from upstairs. This time it truly was Diamond, on the brass bed again. She went up; heaved him off. Had there been a dog curled up and mutinous in the model in Jenny's bedroom? She had a feeling there had been, but no longer trusted either her memory or her senses. Everything was virtual. Diamond wasn't allowed on the bed anyway. She thought perhaps she should tell the police about Jenny Linden's obsession. Everyone knew these things could be dangerous. But now she,

55

Alexandra, had stolen things from Jenny's house. Not the photographs, not the toothbrush – they were hers, if anyone's – but diary and address book. Why had she taken them anyway? She was being dragged into a situation it would be better to ignore. She was exhausted again. She lay down on the brass bed and slept. She was woken by the phone.

8

'Mummy,' said Sascha, in his piercing urgent voice, 'the cat's got kittens. I have to go.' He went.

Irene took the phone.

'Darling,' she said, 'I hope you're not too upset. Men will be men; that is to say, babies.'

'Why should I be upset?' asked Alexandra. 'In particular? Apart from being widowed; all that?'

'You have heard of the Doctrine of Parsimony?' asked Irene.

'No,' said Alexandra. 'Couldn't we talk about the cat having kittens? How many?'

'Eight,' said Irene. 'But where did I go wrong in your education?'

'You sent me to stage school,' said Alexandra.

'The Doctrine of Parsimony is a version of Occam's razor,' said Irene, who had been to Cheltenham Ladies' College in its severe prime and then to Oxford. 'Both suggest that the simplest solution is likely to be the true one; or the most useful. If, as you say, there is a mad woman roaming the edges of Ned's life –'

'His death –' said Alexandra.

'– it is likely that Ned gave her some encouragement. Think of *Fatal Attraction*.'

'But she's so fat and horrid,' said Alexandra.

'You mean why should Ned be interested in her while he had you?'

'Exactly,' said Alexandra. 'Besides, we loved each other. He wouldn't do anything like that. He had a great integrity. He didn't cheapen himself, ever.'

'That's as may be, but you've been away an awful lot,' said Irene. 'Men don't like it. If the wife leaves an empty bed a husband's first impulse is to fill it.'

'I've been working,' said Alexandra. 'What was I supposed to do? It's not my fault if I've had to earn. Ned got me the part in the first place. Do you think I've liked being away from home? We couldn't even have Sascha's fourth birthday on the proper day because I had a matinee. And the poor little boy hated coming up to London at weekends. He missed all his friends' parties, but what could we do? And then Ned died on the dining-room floor, just fell down and died, and I wasn't even there.' She cried.

'Stop blubbing,' said Irene, who'd always wanted to go on the stage but had been thwarted, or so she said, by an early marriage and Alexandra's birth. 'You owe it to your public not to blubber. You'll spoil your looks. And it upsets me. I feel so helpless. I don't like leaving you alone. Likewise, I don't want to bring Sascha back to The Cottage, into such an unhappy house as it must be at the moment.'

'But I miss him,' wept Alexandra.

'Stop thinking about yourself,' said Irene. 'I'll keep Sascha with me until after the funeral, and that's that. It's the best thing. And when is the funeral? Why is nobody saying? Is it going to be a cremation? Really they're the best, except there's always a problem about the ashes.'

'I don't know, I don't know,' wailed Alexandra. 'I can't bear to think about it. Hamish is going to see to all that.'

'You're the widow,' said Irene. 'You really ought to take some responsibility.'

'You've had so much practice, I suppose,' said Alexandra, bitterly. 'You know all about it.'

'Actually,' said Irene, who had indeed buried two husbands out of four, one of them Alexandra's father, 'I do.'

'Was our house full of whispers when my father died? And rustlings, and movements out of the corner of your eyes? Things you thought you almost saw, but didn't really? It's got so spooky here.'

'It was perfectly quiet and ordinary,' said Irene. 'I made sure he died in hospital. But when our cat Marmalade passed away it was just as you describe until she was safely underground. Sascha made a little tombstone in the garden. I expect he told you about that. No? I'd keep seeing Marmalade on the stairs, but when I looked again she wasn't there.

> *As I was going up the stair,*
> *I met a cat who wasn't there,*
> *She wasn't there again today,*
> *I wish to God she'd go away.*

The eyes play tricks. These are Marmalade's eight grandchildren we've just had. I suppose you don't want one for comfort? No? Probably wise. You're never in one place long enough. The sooner Ned is buried the better. Or burned. As for this Jenny Linden, be careful. People like that can be dangerous. If Ned was God what does that make you?'
'Mary?'
'No, darling, the devil. In this Jenny Linden's eyes. Do be careful! Wasn't there a Jenny Linden in *A Doll's House*?'
'Christine Linde,' said Alexandra. 'She plays the doleful widow, a woman who has to earn her own living. Daisy Longriff was playing her – and understudying me. Now Daisy's playing me, and they've got a girl out of wardrobe to do Mrs Linde. Her big chance.'
'That's a bit spooky,' said Irene. Then she had to go because her current husband wanted her to find one of his golf shoes which the puppy had no doubt run off with, and Sascha had tried to put one of the kittens in the dryer. Alexandra, usually so independent, missed her mother and whimpered.

Alexandra put *Mozart's Greatest Hits* on the CD player, very loud. That dispersed a fear or so but added to her melancholy. She put Jenny's diary and address book in a drawer among Ned's papers – then she took them out: there was too much intimacy there – and put them on an open bookcase, where they touched nothing important. She would turn her mind to them when she felt like it. She stored it up in her mind as a kind of treat. Having them in her possession increased her control over the situation. She felt empowered, as would a witch who had just stolen the clippings from her enemy's toenails.

Dr Moebius called. Ned's body would be back in Mr Lightfoot's morgue during the course of the afternoon. He hoped Alexandra did not take his insistence on a full autopsy as unfeeling. It was important that the forensic labs didn't cut corners.

'Only skulls and breastbones,' said Alexandra.

Dr Moebius did not laugh. He repeated that the cause of death was myocardial infarction; he confirmed that there was no sign of cerebral haemorrhage. He asked if Mrs Ludd would like some sleeping pills? He seemed to have forgotten his recommendation of herbal tea.

'What brought my husband's heart attack on?' asked Alexandra. 'So suddenly, and without warning?'

'These things just happen,' said Dr Moebius. 'Or there may have been some undue excitement.'

'Like someone coming to the door you didn't want to see?' suggested Alexandra.

'Possibly,' said Dr Moebius. And he told her that someone you didn't want to see might well increase the heartbeat, and a simple increase could indeed be enough to trigger an infarction. She should think of the many middle-aged men who died when getting up to make an after-dinner speech; or in the middle of sexual congress. He asked when the funeral was, and said he would do his best to get there. Ned had been a charming man, and an excellent patient. That is to say, he seldom came to the surgery. It might have been better if he had come. His blood pressure might have been high for years but no one would know now.

Alexandra said the day of the funeral had not yet been decided.

'Don't leave it too long,' said Dr Moebius. 'An overnight stay at a morgue can cost as much as a five-star hotel. Am I being too practical? I'm sorry.'

'That's OK,' said Alexandra.

Dr Moebius asked when Alexandra was going back to work. She said a week today. He was shocked and said she'd need more time than that – and wasn't there the child to think about? Alexandra said too much thought might be counter-productive: she did not know yet what her financial position was going to be; time off for widowhood might prove an impossible luxury.

'Surely –' said Dr Moebius.

'"Surelys" went out the windows years back,' said Alexandra. 'These days we all do what we have to, not what it would be nice to do if we could.' She asked if Jenny Linden had been in the house when he was called in on the Sunday morning, and Dr Moebius said that was so; apparently she'd turned up to walk the dog and found Ned dead –

'Abbie found him dead,' said Alexandra.

'Oh yes, of course,' said Dr Moebius. 'The one who runs the language school. She was there as well. She's very careful, very responsible. But Mrs Linden was particularly distressed and made quite a nuisance of herself.' He'd given her a sedative and she'd left. If Mrs Ludd happened to see her, would she ask Mrs Linden to drop by to see him? She might find herself suffering from post-traumatic stress disorder.

'Why should she?' asked Alexandra. 'She's not exactly family. Just an acquaintance.'

'She's very sensitive,' said Dr Moebius. 'We are not all made of stone.'

Meaning I am? wondered Alexandra, detecting censure in his voice. She told herself not to be paranoic. Dr Moebius said he had to make an emergency visit to the language school and brought the conversation to an end.

Alexandra called Abbie and told her she'd broken into Jenny's home and how she'd found a shrine to Ned there, and how eerie it was. Abbie said she thought Alexandra had gone mad doing such a thing, but she, Abbie, couldn't come now because the doctor had given the student an injection earlier, and the lad was now reacting to that far worse than to the suspected wasp sting, which had probably never happened, and she'd had to ask the doctor to visit yet again. Should she ask Vilna to go over to The Cottage, if Alexandra was upset?

'No,' said Alexandra. 'I'm just fine, thank you.' Then she asked Abbie if in Abbie's opinion Ned and Jenny had ever had an affair.

Abbie shrieked down the phone and said, 'Why should Ned look at anyone else when he had you?'

61

'He looked at Vilna,' said Alexandra, 'according to Vilna.'

'Vilna's like that,' said Abbie. 'Hopelessly Balkan. She thinks every man's a sexual vampire. Take no notice. What does it matter anyway, Alexandra? Ned's dead. Over. Don't these things fade into perspective?'

'Actually no,' said Alexandra. 'They don't seem to. Since I can't discuss the matter with Ned, or ever have any explanation from him, let alone excuses, or any resolution to do better in future or any apology, and since there is no way more recent times could ever push back past times into irrelevancy, why then no forgiveness is possible. I can't play both sides of the argument on this matter, speaking for him as well as for me. It isn't possible.'

'I don't see why not,' said Abbie. 'If Arthur can play three-dimensional chess with himself, you can forgive a husband post-humously for a trivial and stupid affair –'

'You mean there was one?' Alexandra was quick.

'I mean nothing of the sort,' said Abbie. 'I swear on the cross that to the best of my knowledge and belief nothing untoward happened between Ned and that little bitch Jenny.'

'On the cross?' demanded Alexandra. 'I thought you were a Buddhist.' But she laughed. Then she said, 'Did Ned ever say anything to you about seeing a therapist called Leah?'

'Of course not,' said Abbie. 'If he didn't tell you why would he tell me?'

'You mean he was?'

'Alexandra,' said Abbie. 'Stop all this. You're brooding and para-noic. Can't you just grieve peacefully, and think of the real Ned; do all that stuff you're meant to do: reconciliation and incorporation and all that?'

'I expect I am a little mad,' said Alexandra.

'You certainly are.'

'I'm sorry.'

'What are friends for?' asked Abbie. 'It's OK. Just lean on me.'

9

No sooner had Alexandra put the phone down, having seen Hamish's Citroën coming up the drive, than Abbie had a call from Jenny Linden. Jenny was crying and gulping down the phone and saying she'd got home from her therapist to find someone had broken into her house and stolen her photographs of Ned and her address book and diary.

'What else did they steal?' asked Abbie.

'Nothing,' said Jenny. 'Isn't that enough? To steal what's nearest and dearest to me, at a time like this.'

'Are there signs of a break-in?' asked Abbie.

'Nothing,' said Jenny. 'That's what's so weird. Just Marmalade acting peculiar, miaowing and rubbing up against me. I'm sure he's trying to tell me something. You know Ned gave me Marmalade? She's all I have left of him. No, that's wrong. His spirit is with me. He's in my heart, in my being. Leah said today she felt his presence in me very clearly.'

'That's nice,' said Abbie. 'Are you sure you didn't just put the books somewhere else? It's the kind of thing one does. And you've been so upset. You could have taken down the photos yourself. Have you looked everywhere?'

'The books were on the table when I left,' said Jenny. 'I'll swear they were. But I suppose I could be wrong.'

'Or perhaps you took them with you in the car,' said Abbie. 'And if they were on your lap or something, and when you got out at Bristol they might have fallen out. That once happened to me with my Filofax.'

'I suppose it could be,' said Jenny. 'And I do rotate the photographs, it's true. I could have taken them down and not put the others up. I'm so upset I don't know what I'm doing any more.

The air in my lovely little house was all shaky from spite and malice, I'm sure it was. You don't think Alexandra got in? She is such a hating person. Why should she live and Ned die? There's no justice in the world at all.'

'Now, Jenny,' said Abbie, 'all this is total paranoia. It's guilt speaking, because you used to snoop around in The Cottage from time to time. Ned was Alexandra's, after all. He isn't really yours to mourn. She was his wife.'

'How dare you say such a thing!' cried Jenny Linden. 'Leah says Ned and I were married in heaven: we were old souls reunited at last in this life. Leah realised that the moment she met Ned. She says Alexandra was the cross Ned had to bear: Dave was my cross. Apparently we all have them. What have I got to be guilty about? Nothing! Why are you all so horrid to me? You used to be on my side.'

'Jenny,' said Abbie. 'Now calm down. I think perhaps you tend to remember what you'd like to remember, not what really happened. You must be careful what you say. We don't want anyone to be more upset than they are already.'

'Don't we?' shrieked Jenny Linden. 'Well perhaps I'm sick of bearing things alone. Perhaps I'm tired of being the one good person round here. If I don't get my address book and diary back I'm going to pull the plug on Alexandra Ludd. Stuck-up bitch!'

10

When Hamish stood in the doorway, Alexandra thought for a moment it was Ned. Same build, same colouring: the pale curly hair receding in just the same say. She put her arms round him and felt his warmth; she buried her head in his jacket but he didn't smell of Ned, his body didn't melt into hers. She was conscious of his distress.

'Poor Alexandra,' said Hamish.

'Poor Hamish,' said Alexandra. 'You've been crying. Poor you, poor me.'

She led Hamish into the dining room, pointed to the space between the window and the refectory table, oak, 1860s, which seated eighteen and at whose head Ned had so often sat.

'That was where he died,' she said. 'Just fell down and died. He was watching *Casablanca*; he turned it off ten minutes in, came in here, for air, I suppose: and then clasped his heart and died. At least it was quick.'

'Um,' said Hamish.

'It must have been quick,' said Alexandra. 'I can't bear it not to have been quick. They don't say and I won't ask. I haven't seen the body yet so what do I know? I slept through it, Hamish. How can you sleep through your own husband dying?'

'It would have been more remarkable if you'd woken up,' said Hamish. He was Ned's younger brother, by two years. He lived in Edinburgh, and wore a suit. His wife Sabrina had left him three years ago. He was a senior manager for the Edinburgh Health Authority. Ned would dismiss him as a dull old stick, but sometimes they'd all meet up in London for a meal. Ned and Hamish would talk about their childhood, and Alexandra would feel quite left out. He'd write on occasion to keep Ned in touch with family news – and sent an economical religious greetings card every Christmas and never forgot.

Perhaps he isn't dull at all, thought Alexandra: perhaps it's just another thing Ned said, which I accepted without question. Perhaps now Ned's gone I shall have to go back to the beginning, to where I was when I first met him. Perhaps there are all kinds of things I now think which are really Ned's thoughts, not mine. Judgements I make about people and things, not really mine but Ned's and mine combined. Marriage is a terrible intertwining, a fearful osmosis; I will have to relearn myself.

They went into Ned's study.

'Has someone ransacked the place?' asked Hamish.

Alexandra said no, it always looked like this. The piles of paper made sense to Ned, no doubt, though to others they seemed random. There were shelves of box files but Ned seldom put anything in them. Anything that was there he would take out, in his struggle to locate some missing document, and might not be particularly careful in which file he put it back. She thought there would be life-insurance documents somewhere, and so forth, but she couldn't be sure where. Ned more or less kept up with correspondents; he was always taking letters to the post, but of course, anything difficult or complicated tended to get postponed. Wasn't that the way everyone was?

'No,' said Hamish. He asked Alexandra if she wanted to be consulted about details, or should he simply go ahead and organise what had to be done? He would have to talk to banks, solicitors and so on, and if Alexandra still wished him to organise the funeral, as she had suggested on the phone, he must proceed with that forthwith.

Alexandra said Hamish was a manager by profession: let him go ahead and manage. At the moment she was all over the place: she doubted if she was in her right mind, she was sure Hamish's judgement in most things would be better than her own. He should proceed as he thought fit.

Hamish said he was relieved. He had a week's bereavement leave – a right not officially accorded to siblings, but in the circumstances it had been granted. He would need all that time to get this mess tidied up and in his experience consultation multiplied by at least five the time taken to accomplish anything at all.

'You creative people,' he said, surprising her, 'put too much store by emotion. Emotion doesn't get things done, it doesn't bury the dead. Love can be shown by deeds, not words.' He trembled as he spoke.

'Of course it can,' said Alexandra. 'And I am grateful to you.'

He sat down in Ned's chair; he was the same shape and size as Ned.

'I'm not a particularly creative person,' said Alexandra. 'I'm just on the stage. I get to be flamboyant. Ned was the truly creative one. That's part of the tragedy. His life cut short before he could show the world what he really was! He was writing a stageplay, you know, as well as everything else. But he was such a perfectionist, so self-critical when it came to original work, he found it hard. And all I had to do was say my lines and prance about –'

But Hamish was not listening. He was already shuffling papers, with his back turned to her. It occurred to Alexandra that Hamish could have an opinion of Ned which was not altogether flattering, just as easily as Ned could have of Hamish. If Ned could say, 'My brother? He's a dull old stick,' Hamish could say, 'My brother? Resentful bastard,' and both would have equal weight, in their own circles. The thought shook her.

Hamish called the undertaker, Mr Lightfoot, and arranged a funeral for the following Monday. It was to be at eleven in the morning, and was to last an hour. Mr Lightfoot was to advertise the funeral in the local paper and in *The Times*. Hamish would decide upon the wording. He made an appointment to discuss the type of coffin required and to establish an appropriate level of costs. He called Dr Moebius and went into Eddon Gurney to collect Ned's death certificate and register the death with the part-time Registrar's office there, apologising for the delay. He had the certificate copied at the local stationer's and the copies certified by Sheldon Smythe, Ned's solicitor. All this, once accomplished, he told Alexandra.

'I didn't know Ned had a local solicitor,' said Alexandra, 'let alone one called Sheldon Smythe. But I take your word for it.' Hamish said he'd been named as executor in Ned's will, now in Mr Smythe's possession, which simplified matters. This surprised Alexandra, who seemed to remember that she and Ned had written out mutual wills, as married couples can, each leaving everything to the other, so what need was there of an executor?

Hamish said no doubt Sheldon Smythe, who had been Ned's lawyer for a couple of years, would explain any anomalies at the meeting he had arranged for Tuesday, the day after the funeral. He hoped Alexandra would be feeling more of one piece by then: she would be required to attend.

He wanted Alexandra to make a comprehensive list of such friends and colleagues who would expect to be notified of the time, date and place of the funeral. Time was short: she should make use of the phone, and if necessary get friends to help out. Ned had been a popular man. Hamish, of course, lived a rather quiet life by comparison.

Alexandra said she'd imposed enough upon her friends, but Hamish called Abbie, introduced himself, and explained the problem. Abbie said she'd put her own life to one side and come round with a couple of students. They could work from Ned's address book, if Alexandra was too upset to function.

'Your brother-in-law is a cold fish and a bully,' said Abbie to Alexandra when she came round. 'Ned without charm.'
Alexandra said she didn't care what Hamish's failings were: he was alive, a Ludd, and functioning; she was grateful to him.
'Are we asking Jenny Linden to the funeral?' asked Abbie.

'No, we are not,' said Alexandra. 'Are you mad?'

'She's mad,' said Abbie. 'And it might be safer to ask her than not. She'll come anyway. If you invite her she'll come in a good mood. If you don't, God knows how she'll behave or what she'll say. And the media will be there.'

Alexandra said Jenny Linden came to Ned's funeral over her dead body. Abbie laughed and said she hoped it didn't come to that.

Hamish Ludd spent another four hours in Ned's study going through Ned's papers and making phone calls to Ned's business colleagues. He arranged for Oxfam to come to collect such of Ned's clothes as were recyclable, and for the waste collection to call to take away such as weren't, on the Saturday. Alexandra was to do the sorting. He told her so when she brought him in some coffee. He sat at Ned's desk and the light gleamed off his hair as it had off Ned's. They both had good heads of hair, as had their father and grandfather before them. Scottish engineers, shipyard designers, in the days when there were shipyards.

'I can't do that,' said Alexandra. 'I can't face making decisions. And Ned would be so angry. He collected everything: he hated throwing things away.'

'The sooner it's done the sooner you can restart your life,' said Hamish. 'Get it over. I take it you'll want to stay in this house?'

'Of course I do,' said Alexandra, astonished. 'It's where I and Sascha live.'

'You do have the apartment in London,' said Hamish. 'In Angliss Street. The one Ned owned with Chrissie. You do know about Chrissie?'

'Of course I do,' said Alexandra. 'Ned's first wife. We had to wait for the divorce to come through before we could marry. A dreadful, difficult woman. Why wouldn't I know about her?'

'You're very touchy,' said Hamish. 'I don't know what you do know, and what you don't.'

'I certainly knew about Chrissie,' said Alexandra. 'I had to live with all her things around me when I first moved in with Ned. In fact that's one of the reasons we moved down here. Her spirit was everywhere in Angliss Street, ill-wishing us. It got better with time. I don't even mind being on my own there, these days. I used to, at first.'

'It was her house in the first place,' observed Hamish. 'Why should she go quietly?'

'Ned bought her out,' said Alexandra. 'He was more than fair. They never loved each other. She trapped him into marriage, pretending to be pregnant.'

'Oh yes, yes, yes,' said Hamish. 'All that. Perhaps she miscarried. And then you split the property, sold half at a vast profit, and kept the other half as your *pied-à-terre*. You know there was a still earlier marriage?'

'That's absurd,' said Alexandra. 'Ned may not have told me about Sheldon Smythe because it was simply too boring, but he would certainly have told me all about a marriage. In detail.'

But Hamish said she was mistaken. He had in his possession a letter from Ned dated August 1969, in which he asked his brother to break to their parents the fact that he'd got married. 'He was in Spain that summer,' said Alexandra. 'He went to Paris in 1968, when he was a student, and then went on round Europe.'

'While dull old Hamish stayed behind,' said Hamish, 'and finished his degree. He wrote from Barcelona. Her name was Pilar.'

'Perhaps I'd better see this letter,' said Alexandra.

'It's at home in Edinburgh,' said Hamish, and added that Ned often wrote to him when his life was in crisis.

'I expect he did,' said Alexandra. 'He was a letter person, I was a telephone person.'

'When Ned married Pilar, when he met Chrissie, when he met you, when he divorced Chrissie, when you had your boy. I have all those letters.'

'Then you have something very special to remember him by,' said Alexandra, politely. She could see she was under attack. Perhaps he'd been fond of Chrissie, whom she, Alexandra, had replaced. Such things happened. His eyes were red-rimmed. He had been crying. She felt inclined to forgive him. She asked if he'd ever met this Pilar, and he said no: there'd only ever been the one mention

70

of her, in that particular letter, in August 1969. Ned had returned from Spain on his own, in the summer of 1970.

'I expect she existed in his head,' said Alexandra, 'and even on paper, just not in real life. Or perhaps he just wanted to frighten your parents.'

'I always wondered,' said Hamish. 'Now we'll never know.'

He remarked that in any case he'd found no documents relating to any such marriage or divorce amongst Ned's papers, at least to date.

Alexandra said that might only mean he'd put them in a safe place and then forgotten where, as was his custom. But it could hardly matter now. It had happened, if it had happened, thirty years ago. Presumably Ned was legally married to Chrissie, or he wouldn't have bothered to divorce her to enable him to marry Alexandra. She had been married legally, and widowed legally. She hardly imagined the law relating to marriage was like the law relating to antiques, in which it didn't matter how many times a piece had been sold on: if it had been stolen possession reverted to the original owner. She, Alexandra, had an actor friend who bought a pair of Chinese vases in the Portobello Road for £5,000. He'd used them as props for his portrait in *Hello!*, they'd been recognised as stolen, and he'd had to return them. He ended up minus both vases and £5,000.

'The penalty for vanity,' said Hamish, primly. 'The appetite for publicity to which all theatre people are prone. Your friend should have been more careful. And I believe the same principle does apply in matrimonial law. Any transaction consequent upon an illegal one is invalid.'

'In that case,' said Alexandra, 'we had better be careful not to mention the mythical Pilar in legal circles in case they choose to grow rich at our expense.'

'I can see,' said Hamish, 'that you would find a demotion from second to third wife disconcerting. At least a brother is a brother, and nothing can ever change that.'

'It could certainly change,' said Alexandra, 'if your mother suddenly told you you'd been conceived outside the marriage. You'd become a half-brother overnight.'

Hamish smiled thinly and went back to his brother's papers. Death, thought Alexandra, brings out the worst in everyone, and in this she included herself.

11

Theresa came back from holiday early. She had heard of Ned's death. She brought round a very solid potato and chicken pie as a gesture of condolence and reassurance, and wept quite a lot. Heavy tears fell down her wide, firm, young face. She had burned in the Majorcan sun: she was now bright pink. Grief did not help her complexion. She was very big, her waist as wide as Alexandra's hips, but she had a train of youthful admirers, which she would swat away as if they were flies. She loved only Sascha, she said. Alexandra thanked Theresa for the pie and offers of help, but said she was OK on her own for a bit. Sascha wouldn't be back until after the funeral. She would of course in the meantime pay Theresa her usual wages.

Hamish said, over supper, 'I'm sorry we had our little tiff. We must both make allowances – I can see how upset you are. I never got to know you as well as I would have liked. Ned moved in circles so very different from mine. One makes assumptions about show-business people. You are very brave. And as lovely as your photographs. Just not very organised, and in need of help.' He laid his hand upon her arm. For a moment she was startled, but it was a brotherly and consoling touch and she was appreciative. She was grateful that he'd recovered from his spasm of dislike for her, though she still had no idea what had triggered it. She was just glad he was there in the house. The place stayed quiet, and Diamond slept peacefully, without gasps and snorts of alarm.

Hamish went to bed at ten o'clock. He was tired, as he said, both physically and emotionally. Ned had been his only brother.

Alexandra and Sascha were now his only family. His own had disintegrated. He was, he said, a typical product of the times: living alone, along with twenty-eight per cent of the population. He liked statistics.

It took Hamish an hour to get to bed. To wash, to think, to have a bath, to find soap; he borrowed Ned's pyjamas, which Ned never wore. She could understand that. She'd been wearing one of Ned's shirts all day. That would have to stop, she supposed. Hamish asked for a glass of water. She provided it. He had tucked himself up like a little boy. He looked after her pathetically, as if wanting a bedtime story.

When he had finally settled – worse than Sascha – Alexandra looked through Jenny's address book. She found the address of an 'L. Peacock', in Clifton, Bristol. She looked up Peacock in the directory and found 'Peacock, Leah', and called the number. She counted the rings. Eight. Good. The woman was in bed.
'Hello?' enquired a soft, good-natured voice, though sleepy.
'It's Jenny,' said Alexandra, using Jenny's voice. 'I'm so unhappy.'
'Jenny,' said Leah, 'don't do this to me. I can bear some of your unhappiness, but not all of it.'
'I loved him so much,' said Alexandra/Jenny. 'But he wasn't mine to love.'
'It's the Whispering Guilt again, Jenny,' said Leah. 'Don't listen to it. It means to fill your mind with poison. How many times have we talked about that? I want you to go to sleep. Now what is our sleep word?'
Alexandra put the phone down. She found a 'Dave' in the address book, but he turned out to be a plumber, annoyed at being disturbed. She used Jenny's voice, gave Jenny's address, and asked him to come round in the morning to fix a leak. Early if possible. She called Jenny Linden. It was some time before she answered. Good, again.
'Who is it?'
'This is Ned,' Alexandra whispered. 'From the other side.'
She called the second Dave in the book and got an answerphone.

74

Dave Linden, Theatrical Lighting, freelance. He answered half-way through the message.

'Hi,' said Alexandra brightly. 'This is Alexandra Ludd. I think we met once or twice, at parties. You've been up to The Cottage once or twice. And I think we once met at Lyme Regis.'

'That's right,' he said. 'It's rather late. Do we have to talk now?'

'Yes,' she said. 'We do. I understand your wife suffers from unrequited love for my husband, now dead. That she's been stalking him.'

'I don't know what you mean by unrequited,' he said. 'What was unrequited about it? Why do you think she and I aren't together? I don't want to talk about it. I'm sorry for you, but I don't want you saying bad things about Jenny. She looked up to that bastard you married. He could talk her into anything. She believed everything he told her. I should have gone over and killed him myself; I always wanted to. She wouldn't let me. How could you stand him, a woman like you?'

'I loved him,' said Alexandra.

'And I love Jenny,' he said.

He wept. Alexandra felt mystified. How could a man seriously be in love with dumpy little Jenny Linden?

'I don't want you to do anything nasty to her,' said Dave. 'You're a powerful woman. You could crush her, just like that. I'm not sorry your husband's dead. I'm glad. He ruined my marriage.'

'You don't think,' Alexandra asked, 'that it's all in your wife's head? That she's deluded? Obsessed? That what she tells you simply isn't true? I don't know what she's told you but my impression is it's all fantasy. I was calling you to ask her, for God's sake, to lay off. My husband has just died. I can't cope with your wife's insanity as well. I want you to control her, keep her out of my way. People might even believe the dreadful things she's saying. That Ned and she were having an affair.'

'Why are you doing this to me?' asked Dave Linden. 'It's really warped. Why are you pretending you didn't know what was going on?'

'Nothing was going on except what went on in your wife's head,' said Alexandra. 'You've got to get her on some kind of medication and out of my hair.'

'But they'd grope each other in front of you,' said Dave Linden. 'I saw them. You aren't blind. You must have known. That was what turned them on. You and me having to watch them, having to imagine them together. She said it was her way of getting over it, I wasn't to stop her. It made things worse. But why did you put up with it? Are you sick in the head or something?'

'I never saw them grope each other,' said Alexandra. 'Ned always puts his arms around women. He was just being affectionate.'

'Then they'd dance together,' said Dave Linden, 'and laugh together and look at you and me out of the corners of their eyes and their hands would be everywhere. And you were the one who sent our invitation out. "Dear Dave and Jenny, do come. Ned and I . . ." Through the letter box, down on to the mat: more torture. She'd agree you were a bitch to do it. I'd refuse to go; she'd put the pressure on: "Oh, Dave, oh, Dave, I love him so, let me get it out of my system. Then we'll be together again." So we'd go, and I'd see you watching –'

'Ned always danced close to women,' said Alexandra. 'I never minded. I can't even remember him dancing with Jenny. I'm sure you're right and he did but I don't remember. All this is in your head, Dave. She's told you so many lies.'

'Jenny doesn't lie,' said Dave. 'Jenny never lies. You're the one who's mad, not Jenny. You'd go up to London knowing they'd be together. The moment you'd walk out the door she'd walk in. He died fucking her. He died fucking my wife. Too much excitement. Now leave me alone.'

He put the phone down. Alexandra went to bed. She slept in Sascha's room. She wanted the smell of his soft child's skin in her nostrils: next best thing to having his real presence. Abbie hadn't washed the sheets on Sascha's bed, thank God. It wasn't so much a sleep as a passing-out, unconsciousness forced on her mind.

She woke with the phrase in her head, 'When you walked out she walked in.' Madness. Cold crept round the edges of Sascha's small quilt. She went back to her own bed, and for a moment thought she could feel Ned's warm presence, but it was only Diamond, who had somehow got upstairs again. She did not push him off the bed. Anything warm and alive would do.

12

In the morning, Alexandra called Abbie, and asked Abbie exactly
where the body had lain when she found it. She'd assumed it
was between the table and the window, but on no real grounds,
she could now see. Abbie said Alexandra should try to forget
this kind of detail: wasn't it better to be vague about the matter,
especially since presumably Alexandra would go on living in
The Cottage with Sascha and there was no question of selling?
Though, if Alexandra did, Abbie and Arthur would be interested
in buying: they might sell Elder House and give up the language
school altogether: if she, Abbie, turned her back for a moment
all hell broke loose. But Alexandra must not, must not, believe
Abbie begrudged Alexandra a moment of her, Abbie's, stay at
The Cottage after Ned's death; it was the least she could do for
her friend. She shouldn't even have mentioned 'grudge': of
course it wasn't in her head. Consider that last unsaid, cancel,
cancel. Only five days since the death but it seemed like years.

'Why should someone die of a heart attack?' asked Alexandra.
'Just like that? Wouldn't something have to happen to set it
off?'
Abbie said she didn't know. There was hardly anything death-
inducing in the first ten minutes of *Casablanca*. She repeated
that Alexandra should stop brooding over the detail, forget the
past, and get on with living. Had she had any more trouble
with Jenny Linden? Alexandra said she hadn't. Abbie said she
thought Alexandra should return the address book and diary:
otherwise Jenny Linden might get yet more obsessive and
send in the police. What, as a matter of interest, was in the
books?

'Nothing much,' said Alexandra. 'What you would expect from someone with such a little life?'

There was a short silence and then Abbie said, 'You shouldn't talk about people like that, Alexandra. As if you were something special but they were nothing. I can see people could get infuriated.'

Alexandra was hurt. She supposed that if you didn't have a husband to add a kind of veracity to your life, to bolster up your opinions – well, opinions that you and your husband shared; a general world-outlook, as it were, acquired over time – you might well find yourself under attack. She and Ned together were entitled to a general superiority, an assumption of centrality in relation to those around, but on her own it was a different matter.

'I just mean,' said Abbie, 'that Jenny could cause a lot of trouble, so please go carefully. Don't stir things up, Alexandra, if you can help it.'

'What sort of trouble?' asked Alexandra. 'Who's going to believe her?'

'You know what people are,' said Abbie.

'I'm beginning to,' said Alexandra, and Abbie had to go because one of the students had spilled calligraphy ink over the table-cloth. The student had been making her, Abbie, a Happy Cherry Blossom card to demonstrate the tender customs of the Japanese in their home country as compared to the brutality of other nations abroad. It was just a pity she was doing it on a white tablecloth.

Alexandra called Vilna.

'Vilna,' she said. 'I think I'm being given the run-around by Abbie.'

Vilna said if that was the case it was only for Alexandra's good. Abbie adored Alexandra. Alexandra asked Vilna where exactly in the dining room the body had been when she arrived at The Cottage and Vilna said Alexandra should think about the future not the past and start life again. Abbie had put a blanket over the corpse; she, Vilna, had never seen a dead body: that's why she'd had to go down to the morgue to see it without its blanket.

79

'I hope you enjoyed the sight,' said Alexandra, and slammed down the phone. Then she had to call Vilna back to apologise. A friend was a friend. Vilna said it was OK: the English had such a funny view of death it kept surprising her but she was adjusting to it. Would Alexandra like to use her house for the party?

'Party?' asked Alexandra.

'After the funeral,' said Vilna. 'I think you call it a wake.'

Alexandra accepted the offer.

13

In the morning Alexandra took Jenny's small blue address book and diary into the little stationer's in Eddon Gurney. The shop was two doors down from the morgue. She could feel Ned lying there, but could not picture his appearance. She too had never seen a dead body. Her father had died in America; her mother had not encouraged her to go to the funeral.

'You'll only upset his widow,' Irene had said. It was clear that serial marriage made a mockery of funerals. The divorced spouse, denied the partner in life, was also denied any conventional solace that related to the death. With the death of the distant parent, the forgotten and unacknowledged child finds himself, herself, with even less substance than before: with even fewer rights to any existence at all. The ghosts of the departed wave to others but not to us; those who are rejected in life are rejected in death, and there is no healing it. Ned had not turned to look back at Alexandra as he went into the forest.

'So sorry,' Angela Paddle was saying to Alexandra. She and her husband Reg Paddle ran the stationer's shop. Reg had left the Army and used his money to set up the business. His belief was that every small town and village in the country these days needed its communication centre, and riches would come to those prescient enough to provide a copier, a fax, and a computer-plus-modem to the community. But few in Eddon Gurney had much interest in the outside world, other than those in what Mr Lightfoot called 'the Bohemian Belt'. Angela Paddle wore a scratchy beige sweater with no blouse underneath. She seemed not to understand comfort, but her face was kind. 'So sorry. A great shock.'

81

'A great shock,' said Alexandra. 'Could you do me copies of these?' and she handed over her trophies. She could see how unlikely it seemed that they were hers. These were not the personal records of anyone with many friends, or a great deal of occupation. She did not even want them thought of as hers. 'My brother-in-law is up at The Cottage putting Ned's affairs in order. We need these addresses and so forth for the funeral invitations.' Her voice faltered. Why was she explaining? Never apologise, never explain, Ned would advise. Which was, she supposed, just as well. He was certainly now in no position to do either.

Angela Paddle looked both reluctant and doubtful. This was her custom when anyone asked her to use the new technology.
'We don't usually do anything bound,' she said. 'But you must be upset. I'll do my best. Funny to think of your husband lying on that slab just a couple of doors down.'
'Very funny,' said Alexandra.
'I'll pop in and see him later,' said Angela Paddle.
'You do that,' said Alexandra.
'Better to see it for real than think about it. Mrs Linden's just been to see him for the third time,' said Angela Paddle. 'Doing her best for him. The living need to watch by the dead. Strange how times change. When I had my baby it was unheard of to have a man around at the birth. Now it's all but compulsory. Same with the dead. Once they kept bodies out of the way, tried not to think about them. Now everyone wants to see.' She broke into a hymn:

> '*Be there at our closing*
> *And give us we pray*
> *Your peace in our hearts, Lord*
> *At the end of the day.*'

'Yes, give us peace,' said Alexandra, and thought this strange and dreadful woman might yet be the one to make her cry.

'Mr Lightfoot's a good man,' said Angela Paddle. 'I wouldn't want to do a job like that, for all everyone treats it like nothing.'

'No, you just stick to faxes,' said Alexandra. 'So Jenny Linden was in, was she? She's not a very close friend of ours.'

'She said she was,' said Angela Paddle. 'And a colleague of Mr Ludd's, and there when he died. What a shock for the poor woman.'

'Jenny Linden is obviously very upset,' said Alexandra, 'and very imaginative at the best of times. I don't think you should take too much notice of what she says. My husband was alone when he died.'

'That's right,' said Angela Paddle. 'He died in the night, didn't he, and you were in London in that play of yours about the doll. I couldn't make too much sense of Mrs Linden. You know how some women get: all over the place, gulping and sobbing. I just thought it was good of her to sit by the body so much.'

'Of course it is,' said Alexandra. 'The more the merrier. I might go and sit myself. I'll be back in a couple of hours, for the copies.'

'It won't be cheap,' said Angela Paddle.

'I bet it won't be,' said Alexandra cheerfully.

Alexandra called in down the road to see Mr Lightfoot. She didn't have to repark the car, the morgue was so close. He took her to view the body. Fortunately, there was no one else there doing the same thing. He asked her what she wanted Ned to wear for the cremation. He'd had a phone call from the deceased's brother, suggesting a cremation. Now he wanted to confirm with the widow that Mr Hamish Ludd was the proper person for him to deal with. Mrs Linden had been in, wanting to know whether there would be an interment. A burial, that was.

'What has Mrs Linden to do with it?' asked Alexandra.

'The poor lady's very upset,' said Mr Lightfoot. 'A little bit unbalanced, the way people get. I take no notice. You're the widow, that's the main thing.'

Alexandra stared at Ned's body and could see that she must take charge of the situation. She had never held 'truth' in much regard; it seemed to her a thing which shifted with the times, unreliable as any kind of fixed goal. She was an actor: she would find the truth of a role one night, and a wholly different truth the next. Both would work. She understood the slipperiness of words. She knew that those who protested often protested too much. She knew that definitions limited rather than explained: that once you had onion-peeled away opinion and thought you had arrived at a firm layer of truth, that layer went too, to reveal mere sponginess underneath. In the end you didn't want truth, you just needed to know what had happened.

'Mr Lightfoot,' she asked finally, directly, 'where exactly was the body when you arrived?'

'On the floor,' said Mr Lightfoot. 'With a blanket over it.'

'I know,' said Alexandra. 'But where on the floor?'

'Oh well,' said Mr Lightfoot, 'truth's truth. At the top of the stairs.'

Alexandra took this in.

'Why did my friends say it was in the dining room?'

'Artistic people have their own habits,' said Mr Lightfoot. 'How do I know? All this breaking through, making one room out of two. The front parlour's a thing of the past, as I know to my cost.'

'Ned fell down at the top of the stairs?'

'He died in his own bed,' said Mr Lightfoot, 'as a man should. Then your friend from the language school tried to carry him downstairs for reasons of her own, but a warm body's hard to move, as she soon found out. So she left him at the top of the stairs covered with a blanket.'

'Who was in the house when you arrived?' asked Alexandra.

'Why don't you think about the future, Mrs Ludd? Put the past behind you? It's what I always recommend.'

'Was Jenny Linden there?'

'I'll say she was! Rushing round naked like a headless chicken. Throwing herself all over the body as we tried to get it out. Women will do that, of course, in these circumstances. And the dog barking and barking as the dawn comes up. No one had thought to take him for a walk. I found a nightie and put it on her, to make her decent.'

'Ned was asleep in bed,' said Alexandra. 'He heard a noise; he

84

turned on the light, sat up. And there was Jenny Linden in the room. Jenny Linden has been harassing and persecuting my husband, Mr Lightfoot. She's quite mad. He tried to get her to leave, but she wouldn't. He lost his temper with her – and that's when he had a heart attack.'

'I expect that's how it went,' said Mr Lightfoot.

'Don't be tactful with me,' shouted Alexandra. 'That's how it did go. Then she took off her clothes to make the most of it, to make everyone believe –'

Ned's body seemed to be radiating a kind of cold blue light. But perhaps it was only the reflection of Mr Lightfoot's neon lights off Ned's now waxy skin. Did all the blood flow out during an autopsy? Or, deprived of life and movement, did the blood congeal, and shrink and harden? Alexandra tried not to look at the corpse too much: it seemed such a mockery of the real thing. An object offered in replacement: a fake, someone's attempt to deceive. The real Ned had walked off into the forest; he had not looked behind. He had not even wanted her to go with him.

'She killed him,' said Alexandra. 'That mad woman killed my husband.'

'I didn't hear that,' said Mr Lightfoot. 'You have to be careful what you say. There's such a thing as slander. I've seen a lot in my time but I've never seen anyone as upset over a death as poor Mrs Linden.'

'I'm the widow,' said Alexandra.

'You took your time acknowledging it,' said Mr Lightfoot. 'Every time a body's viewed something goes out of it, but that's just my opinion. Now you're finally here, I'll leave you alone with your husband. What's left of him.'

He sauntered off, gaunt and dusty in his badly-cut tweedy black trousers. Practice with the bereaved, competence over death, knowledge of what others would rather not contemplate, earned him a surface of worldly self-confidence, which he oiled with a veneer of spite. He was still an Untouchable, Alexandra consoled herself. People, recognising the undertaker or his wife, moved away in the supermarket, not wanting any suggestion of physical contact. Birds of ill-omen. Crows.

'Ask Dr Moebius,' said Mr Lightfoot, turning back. 'He's the one to ask, not me. I could tell it was a heart attack; short but violent; unmistakable. Why he wanted all that business with the autopsy beats me.'

'I expect he just wanted to keep standards up,' said Alexandra.

'Running bodies around here and there,' Mr Lightfoot said. 'It isn't right. Not much is right about death, these days. In some places they bury the coffins vertically, even though that adds to the digging costs.'

Alexandra sat on a hard chair by the body and stared into space. Ned kept her a kind of implacable company. She didn't cry. There were two witnesses to the death. One was Ned and he was dead. The other was alive but unreliable. She would like to preserve what dignity she could for Ned, herself, and Sascha. She gave up and drifted into inorganic suspension until it was time to collect the documents from Angela Paddle. She was charged £20, which she thought exorbitant, but did not argue.

Alexandra returned the originals to Jenny Linden. She parked her car around the corner from Eddon Gurney prison. A homely little red car was parked outside Jenny's house. Alexandra recognised it as Jenny's: she'd seen it around often enough, here and there, even in The Cottage yard. She walked casually by the house, in the road, her face averted from the window. When she got to the car she dropped the documents on the ground, on the driver's side. Jenny Linden would be puzzled to find them but would have to make up some story for herself which would solve the problem: they'd fallen out when she opened the door; they'd been there all the time. Whatever. If Jenny's distress was as great as everyone said she wouldn't be in a condition to give the matter too much attention. It wouldn't occur to her that copies had been made, that Alexandra now had some undefined power which gave her access to Jenny's world, as Jenny apparently had into her, Alexandra's, world.

86

Alexandra got home to find Hamish worrying about the S to Z's in Ned's address book. Abbie had been dilatory; so had Alexandra; there were people yet to be contacted. Alexandra spent an hour or so on the phone going through these last pages, telling friends and strangers the date and time of the funeral. Some knew of Ned's death, some didn't. Some groped for consoling words to say to her. Some needed her consolation. It was exhausting. At the end she was no more convinced of Ned's death than she had been at the beginning. She kept hearing his voice in her ear, and jumping. But it was Hamish's voice, on the office phone, in another room. Muted, it had the same timbre as Ned's.

As dusk fell the same bats came wheeling out of the old barn in the same way as they always had. Their world had not changed at all: why should it? Perhaps what one mourned for people was that they were no longer there to observe familiar things. Everyone died. It was a terrible system: to plant in the mind the possibility of permanence and then snatch it away.

Of course Ned had not been having an affair with Jenny it was dreadful that the thought had been put into her head in the first place. Dave Linden had been driven mad by his wife: he had been fed false information, rendered wretched, and was stupid, stupid, stupid to begin with. Everyone knew that. All she had to face was that Jenny Linden had got as far as the bedroom and been the one to find the body. Which was bad enough.

Alexandra called Leah; again using Jenny Linden's voice.
'It's me,' she sobbed. 'It's me.'
'Be strong and calm,' recommended Leah. 'I'll be able to fit you in tomorrow. I've had a cancellation. Let the wife do the earthly part the way she wants: it's nothing. So the body rots, or the body burns, what's the difference? You and Ned continue on your spiritual path together.'
'Can you give me a key phrase?' begged Alexandra/Jenny. She remembered that from something Ned had once said. What was it?

'Worst fears,' murmured Leah. 'Worst fears,' and put the phone down.

Worst fears.

What did the woman mean by 'worst fears'? Was the phrase some kind of therapeutic aide to a peaceful mind? In which the client was meant to envisage the worst that could happen, and because the present didn't match up to that, feel better?

What would Jenny Linden's worst fears be? If she, Alexandra, was acting Jenny in a play, what would it feel like? How would it go?

Alexandra took Diamond for a walk in the fields at the back of The Cottage. This is how it went.

Here am I, Jenny Linden, a woman in my mid-forties, my life passing by; loved by a husband who loves me whatever I do, therefore able to do whatever I like and not lose income. I have a little life. I sit in a little house, in a small town, reducing what is large to what is small. The future shrinks, along with the present. I love the theatre, as so many do who have an unsatisfactory life, or feel the need for its enrichment. I am by nature a fan: the extreme example of fan being the one who shot John Lennon; the only way to own his hero wholly being to cause his death. If I can obsessively worship, I can also obsessively destroy.

By chance I, Jenny Linden, have become the fan of one Ned Ludd, a minor celebrity in the outside world, but in the world in which all my yearnings are fixated, that of the theatre. I want him to take notice of me. I have no real view of myself, so it seems to me possible that, if I play my cards right, that my love for him, my obsession with him, will work some kind of magic so he will reciprocate.

I am eaten up with envy for his wife, who is beautiful, worldly, successful, has media attention and press cuttings to show for it. She is so confident I hate her. What does she have that I haven't? I'll show her. I will make myself useful to Ned: walk his dog, do his research for free, worm my way into his life; at his death grieve so hard and so publicly the world will believe that we were intimately related, the better to humiliate his widow. I will steal her happy memories: I will disturb and upset her, fill her mind with doubts. If I have no happy memories, neither will she.

Jenny Linden's worst fears? Now Ned Ludd's dead? That Alexandra will be revenged on me. That she will damage me, or mine. Stop my husband loving me: now Ned's gone, I'll need him. That she will somehow bring me to the realisation that Ned Ludd pitied me but scarcely thought of me, let alone loved me.

Worse, worse, worse. That even Alexandra Ludd can't be bothered thinking about me; negates me by ignoring me.

Worst fears:
Mine, Alexandra Ludd's worst fears.
Can I get to this? Be the actress impersonating me?
How would I see myself then?

My worst fear used to be that Ned would die and leave me alone to reinterpret a world so long and well interpreted through his eyes. Man and wife grow together, sop up each other's natural juices, there is no avoiding it: if there is a child grown in her it is the joint essence of them both: the character and nature of the child infects the mother, and through the mother the father too. Thus the unit is sealed together, bonded without, suffusing within. This is why death or divorce is so shattering: wrench out a piece of the whole and what's left is like a raw shank of beef hanging in the kitchen bleeding. The child feels it just as much. It's the sharing of the bed does it, thought Alexandra. There should be more separate beds, separate bedrooms, coming untos –

89

How lovely the evening was. She could look back and see the two chimneys of The Cottage showing over the ridge. If she retraced her steps it would reveal itself to her, little by little. That familiar solid structure, waiting patiently for her return, holding its breath: child and mother both: home. You could not love a house as you loved a person, of course not, but you almost could. Old houses acquired personalities, the sum of all who had lived in them. Mended, painted, refreshed, cleaned, they glowed at you, acknowledged you; spick and span, they made you dance; neglected, took your pocket money. Ned was gone, but lived on in the roof, the stone, the beams that had absorbed his attentions; which had often made him groan, as a parent will a child who overspends but still is loved. The climbing roses Ned had planted at the foot of the house, now mingled with the leaves of the Virginia creeper, crept higher and higher; their great red sensuous globes hung beneath the eaves. Ned was gone but they went on; blooming, fading, falling, renewable, as Ned was not. The broad beans on their pyramids swelled and grew big and tough without him: but now at least would survive to seed themselves. So much of what Ned did continued. She, Alexandra, lived; the house and garden were now both her consolation and her obligation. She must remember the woodworm in the settle: do something before it spread. All it needed was injecting, minute hole by minute hole, minuscule death-dealing to minuscule enemies.

Home, and all that went with it: where Sascha had been conceived and born; where Ned, in spite of all, had held her, loved her, nurtured her, as she had him. So many meals cooked, so many friends welcomed, so much good conversation. The books on the shelves, the familiar, exhilarating life of the mind, the world's attention focused here, the conclusions of mankind dissected; the laughter exchanged, the wonders explained, marvels revealed. A good marriage; a good place to be, to have been. Where there are angels there will be devils too. Woodworm, Jenny Linden, crows nesting in the chimneys, greenfly, bad reviews, rejected manuscripts; minuscule enemies in comparison. The furniture, the precious pieces, Ned's and her pride, built up over years, dusty finds in antique shops, shoddy bits from junk stalls, rescues from skips, neglected pieces inherited, which she and he would restore, beeswax-polish until they glowed with richness revealed; as if the pieces themselves acknowledged their rescue and lived again and were grateful. Memories were the real treasure: these no one could rob you of.

She wished she could remember more about the day at Kimmeridge Bay. Quite an outing, quite a party. Had her mother been there? Sascha and she had found a fossil ammonite, almost perfect: its simple spirals formed 500 million years ago. Ned had had it polished and it was kept on the marble mantelpiece in the living room: where Ned had been watching *Casablanca*. Ten minutes of it. Then changed his mind.

Worst fears.

Alexandra put her mind back to them: she made herself. Ned has died. I am bleeding. I have the past, but no present; yet I will make a future.

If I were an actress impersonating me, if I was getting to the root of me, if I was doing, as a dramatic exercise, the worst fears, highest hopes part, I would say my worst fear is that Jenny Linden is not insane, that Ned and she were having an affair, that she was in bed with him, in our brass bed into which he had invited her, and that he died fucking her, so great was his excitement and pleasure. That for a time the jerks and pantings of the dying man echoed the jerks and pantings of a joy which once I thought was reserved for me but was not; and stopped, and he was dead.

There, it is said. It is the simplest thing to believe, and therefore probably true. The Doctrine of Parsimony. Occam's razor. Thank you, Mother.

That Jenny Linden eased herself out from under my husband – does an erect penis go limp in death, or stiffen harder? To find out I would have to ask her, and I cannot bring myself to ask that. She would stare aghast at the clawing hand which so recently pleasured her, the popping eyes which just a while ago were clouded with passion and intent and now were blank, and she fell or crawled out of the bed. Wondered no doubt for a moment whether to leave like a thief in the night, but decided that the drama was too tempting to be left, and called Abbie.

'Oh, Abbie, Abbie, come at once. A terrible thing has happened. Ned's died in my arms.'

And perhaps, who knows, her husband Dave.

'Oh, Dave, Dave, what will I do? The man I love is dead. I'm so unhappy. Now I only have you.'

And Dave hadn't come, but Abbie had. She came round at once, decided I, Alexandra, had to be saved, swore Jenny to secrecy, dragged the body off the bed as lately and repeatedly Alexandra had dragged Diamond, got the limp and heavy thing as far as the top of the stairs, couldn't continue, covered the body with a blanket, called the doctor, called me, Alexandra, called Mr Lightfoot, calmed Jenny as best she could, called Vilna to get Jenny out of the house, watched the body carried on the stretcher to Mr Lightfoot's ambulance. Abbie had taken the sheets from the bed and laundered them – what was on them: semen, blood, spittle, urine, excreta? Presumably everything burst out from a dying man. Was the stored semen gone or about to go when death intervened? Abbie the good friend. She'd know. Jenny would know. Alexandra would never know. She'd never ask.

Worst fears. There, that's over. Nothing worse than that. Unless perhaps Jenny Linden was on top of Ned, not beneath. He liked that. It would have been nice if that had been reserved for me.

Saving graces.

None of it was like this at all. That Ned heard a noise in the night and got out of bed where he lay alone and peacefully, missing me, Alexandra, whom he loved, and found Jenny the madwoman in the house, had been alarmed, and had therefore died where he stood. (Yes, and that Abbie just put the sheets through the wash as a kind of nervous domestic tic.)

That Ned might have bedded Jenny Linden, if he did, not because he planned to but on the spur of the moment. (Yes, and had left Sascha with Irene and not joined Alexandra in London because he really did have work to do.)

Or perhaps Jenny Linden was blackmailing him, or she had hypnotised him, or he thought if he did it once she'd give up and go away in peace. (Yes, and Jenny Linden was an alien from outer space.)

And Ned was so overcome with guilt he had died mid-illicit-fuck. (Yes, and she'd tied him down and raped him.)

Worst fears:
That she, Alexandra, had been deceived by Ned in his life: that the grief she felt for him was wholly compromised, so it would never heal, never go away, because she had no idea what she was grieving for. And not knowing, and never being able to know, there was no 'her' at all. That was the truly worst fear: her own non-existence. She was something elusive, a conjuror's effect, produced by the trickery of someone, for the entertainment of others.

Which was what she did for a living, come to think of it. A living despised even as it was earned. Or as Ned would say, 'The theatre would be OK if only it wasn't for the bloody actors. Not you, my darling. Present company excepted.' As if it ever was.

Worst fears:
That God was not good. That the earth you stood upon shifted, and chasms yawned; that people, falling, clutched one another for help and none was forthcoming. That the basis of all things was evil. That the beauty of the evening, now settling in a yellow glow on the stone of The Cottage barns, the swallows dipping

93

and soaring, a sudden host of butterflies in the long grasses in the foreground, was the lie: a deceitful sheen on which hopeful visions flitted momentarily, and that long, long ago evil had won against good, death over life. She who had flickered a little for Ned's entertainment, brightly, to Ned's temporary advantage, was herself as sour and transitory as the rest of a foul creation. That in receiving Ned's flesh into her body, so often and with such powerful awareness of love – so that it seemed to be far more than physical excitation and a sacrament, a connection through to the source of the universe, the light which suffused all things, and was there, if you had eyes for it, in the glow of the sun against the stone walls, as well as in the dancing of butterflies – that in this she had been mocked.

Best remembrance:
That it had happened, that connection, that joy, when, on the Monday night before he left London she and Ned had made love, not just sex, not just fucking; love. That was the truth of it. Afterwards he had looked straight into her eyes; Ned's soft look, and said, 'I do love you.' She would hold to that. (Yes, but why the 'do' – as if there had ever been doubt of it? And why did Ned sometimes say to friends, 'Oh, Alexandra: so unobservant for such a clever person.' Well?)

Worst understanding: that Ned was no longer alive, for her to put these points to him, for him to put his arms around her, and hers round him, and in the sure warmth of that touch for them both to be reborn, in hope. He was gone for ever: she was here alone.

Alexandra turned and walked home to face whatever had to be faced. Diamond was reluctant to go back. He wanted to walk for ever.

14

Hamish, Abbie and Vilna were sitting at the kitchen table when she and Diamond got home. Hamish was at the head of it, pouring tea carefully and precisely, unused to such an activity. Tea no doubt was normally something poured for him, in a living room. Hamish was a cup-and-saucer man, not a mug in the kitchen man. But he appeared to like being here, doing this. Hamish seemed to Alexandra to be like a small boy allowed to take the steering wheel of the family car and pretend to be in charge. She wondered to what degree Hamish had envied Ned. And Abbie her friend and Vilna, Abbie's friend and her own familiar and surely harmless acquaintance, seemed suddenly not quite so trustworthy as she, Alexandra, had thought. They were sitting at her table as of right, but not invited: she felt wary. She wanted them to go, but how could she say so? They were her friends: this was her future family. When men died, or went, the women friends moved in to close the gap: consolatory comfort, female friends. That's what friends were for.

She didn't want to talk, she wanted to go to bed, but the brass bed was compromised, even by thought, by the merest contemplation of Jenny Linden's occupancy of it, of Ned's arms around Jenny Linden, even temporarily, even by mistake, even under duress, even regretted as occurring; Jenny Linden's naked flesh against Ned Ludd's, forget the violence of his dying: a just penalty, you could see, for the violence of his own act against the heart of the universe. Summon up the Devil, the Devil gets you – forget the body lying in the morgue, so much life and passion reduced to a marble penis forever firm against an icy groin – there could be no forgiveness. None. Her bed.

'You look like a ghost,' said Vilna.

'That's Ned's province,' said Alexandra, and laughed.

'This always was a house of laughter,' said Hamish. There was silence.

Then Alexandra said to Abbie:

'Do you really think Jenny Linden's mad?'

'No,' said Abbie.

'Do you?' asked Alexandra of Vilna.

'No,' said Vilna.

Alexandra was glad they had given up pretending but wondered why they had decided to do so. She felt that some extra betrayal of her, Alexandra, gave them new pleasure. Their secret had given them power over her. Now they chose to exercise that power.

'At least none of you have to pretend any more. I know Jenny Linden was with Ned when he died. They were in the bed together upstairs.'

She waited for them to deny it, but no one did. Not even Hamish. Worst Fears realised. Her survival now depended on Best Remembrance.

Hamish said, 'I was telling them of the dreadful time you nearly went off with Eric Stenstrom, and how upset Ned was. He really loved you at the time.'

'How do you know about me and Eric Stenstrom?' asked Alexandra, taken off guard. 'Only Ned knew that.'

Both Abbie and Vilna took in little sharp breaths, as if they'd been waiting to take them. Confirmation!

'Not that there was anything really to know,' Alexandra amended, quickly. Perhaps rather too quickly. 'And what do you mean, Ned loved me "at the time". Really, Hamish!'

There seemed to be shadows of Ned working through Hamish's face, looking for a home. The eyebrows were the same, the set of the jaw. The family resemblance seemed stronger now Ned was no longer there in the flesh to deny it. Alexandra realised she had probably in the past seldom been in a room with Hamish in which Ned was not there too.

'As for that time I "nearly went off with Eric Stenstrom",' remarked Alexandra, 'I certainly know nothing about it, nobody told me, how come you seem to know more than me?'

Why was she having to defend herself in her own home? Who were these people?

'Ned and I exchanged letters from time to time,' said Hamish. 'As you know. We didn't get to see each other much but we were very close. There's a letter from him to me about you and Eric Stenstrom.'

'He shouldn't have written about it, and you shouldn't have spoken about it,' said Alexandra. 'These things are private.'

'These are your friends,' said Hamish. 'Surely there's no harm in their knowing? And surely you don't resent Ned writing to me? His brother? Wives don't own husbands. And men aren't without feeling, in spite of what you women like to say. If women claim the right to women's talk, you can hardly grudge men their men talk.' Alexandra perceived again, and clearly, that Hamish simply didn't like her. She said nothing, but from now on wanted not to confide in him. She did not think there was any real damage he could do her, but she must think before she spoke.

'Anyway,' said Abbie, in her light, polite tones, 'Vilna and I knew about Eric Stenstrom already.'

'Such a good-looking man,' said Vilna, in her most slurred and earthy voice. 'I do envy you, darling. It's the buttocks. I like a Hamlet with good buttocks.'

Eight years back Eric Stenstrom had played Hamlet in a Hollywood movie, dressed in tights more suitable for a ballet dancer on a stage a long way from the audience. He had regretted it but it had not been forgotten.

Hamish, Abbie and Vilna had been drinking wine. They had taken it without asking. It was the Barolo Ned most treasured, the '86. They had formed a kind of cabal against her.

'Jenny Linden came over this afternoon,' said Abbie, 'and told me all about you and Eric Stenstrom. So you really shouldn't be shocked and surprised if Ned had his own entertainments. It's hypocritical of you, Alexandra.'

'What could Jenny Linden possibly know about me and Eric Stenstrom?' asked Alexandra.

'What Ned told her,' said Abbie.

'I don't believe that,' said Alexandra.

'Never trust a man, darling,' said Vilna.

Alexandra said she was tired, and suggested Abbie and Vilna leave. They did. Hamish had the spare room. She no longer wanted to sleep in her own bedroom. She slept again in Sascha's bed. It occurred to her that perhaps Abbie and Vilna, like Hamish, had their own reasons for being resentful.

No. That way madness lay. Abbie was her friend; Vilna trying to be her friend. She, Alexandra, was exhausted and paranoic, and saw nightmares where none were, and in the morning everything would seem different. But it was a pity Eric Stenstrom's name had come up.

15

Alexandra woke early; birdsong was loud in the dawn. At seven-thirty there was a knock on the front door. Alexandra went down to answer it, in her blue and white silk dressing gown, Ned's favourite. Presently, she thought, she would have to buy new clothes, so that everything didn't keep relating back to Ned. She thought it would be the postman, wanting her to sign for a parcel, but it was Jenny Linden. She stood on the threshold, glum but defiant. She'd put on lipstick, though not very well. Her mouth looked lopsided. She wore a nondescript padded jacket which made her look four-square, and a pleated skirt ten years out of date.

'I've come to take Diamond for a walk,' Jenny Linden said. She brushed past Alexandra and went through to the kitchen. She unlocked the utility-room door, apparently accustomed to the difficulty with the lock – you had to push before you pulled – and called Diamond. Diamond staggered out, fresh from sleep, and seeing Jenny, leapt up at her, instantly expectant.

'Walkies,' said Jenny Linden.

'Get out of my house,' said Alexandra.

'Please can't we be friends?' asked Jenny Linden, pathetically. 'I hate you being so hostile to me. If I meet aggression I go completely to pieces. We've both of us lost Ned. I'm holding on by a thread. Please be nice to me.'

'No,' said Alexandra.

Jenny Linden began to turn nasty. Her voice went even softer. 'But I made Ned happy,' she said, 'in the last days, his last hours, while you were off in London with Eric Stenstrom. But you don't care about that, you only care about yourself. You don't know what love is.'

'You're polluting my house,' said Alexandra. 'Get out of it.'

'You're so self-centred,' said Jenny Linden. 'I used to defend you but I see now Ned was quite right. And where's Sascha? Don't tell me you've just shuffled him off again? Is he with your mother? The Romanoff of the Golf Course? That's what Ned always called her. Not even him being dead makes a dent in you, does it? The gloss is so hard. You ought to have treatment, Alexandra. You're not fit to be in charge of that child.'

'I don't know where you get all this information,' said Alexandra, 'but it certainly wasn't from Ned. It's all just sleazy gabble, and evil. As for Eric Stenstrom, he's gay, and everyone knows it.'

'That's not what Ned said,' positively whispered Jenny Linden. 'And why are you so defensive? Are you feeling guilty or something? I'm really sorry for you, Alexandra. You must be feeling ever so bad. I expect what happened is that you were in bed with your Eric when Ned died in my arms.'

'It won't work,' said Alexandra. 'You're not going to lure me into any kind of discussion about anything. Just go away or I'll call the police.'

'I'd have a thing or two to tell them,' said Jenny Linden. 'Call away.'

Alexandra lifted her hand to strike the other woman, but Diamond growled. Diamond growled at Alexandra. Alexandra's hand fell.

'Diamond knows the truth of it,' said Jenny Linden, smiling a smug little smile, her plump bottom in its dreadful skirt wedged against the Ludds' kitchen table. 'Diamond knows what you're like. Animals always know. When you want to talk to me, Alexandra, in a calm and friendly way, you know where to find me. Ned brought you round to visit me in my studio once. I was rather flustered; I hadn't expected it. He and I had only been out of bed about twelve hours. Well, twelve hours and twenty minutes. I was still sore. Ned could be quite vigorous, couldn't he? Perhaps he wasn't when he was with you: he said I was the only one really turned him on. Don't believe me if you don't want to. It's true.'

'I don't believe you.'

'We'd had this argument: he said you were so insensitive to atmosphere you'd never even guess; I said I didn't believe that, you were an actress; he said actresses were as thick between the ears as they were between the legs.'

'Actors,' said Alexandra, automatically.

'So he brought you round to my place, took me by surprise, and he was right, you didn't notice a thing. Not even when we went out together to look at photographs and you stayed behind and stroked Marmalade and looked bored. He was right about that too. You can do a lot in three minutes if you're really turned on; if it's dangerous.'

'My mother had a marmalade cat,' said Alexandra. It seemed her mind could only react to detail.

'Marmalade's one of her kittens,' said Jenny Linden. 'Ned gave him to me. Why did you take my photographs away? Ned liked me to have them. It doesn't make any difference. I've got lots more and they're there in my heart anyway. Sealed in memory. You can't take that away from me. And Mrs Paddle told me: you made copies of my diary, and address book. I was angry at first; not now. It just keeps you closer to me. Connected, like. We'll be friends in the end. We're part of each other, through Ned. I think you ought to try and be nice to me. I can make life a whole lot nastier for you if I choose.'

'Piss off,' said Alexandra.

Jenny Linden smiled at Alexandra. This time Alexandra hit her: a hard slap on the cheek. Jenny wailed and ran off, a dumpy little thing pottering on too small feet. Alexandra hoped she would overbalance. Then Alexandra would jump on Jenny Linden and kick her to death. But Jenny kept going. Diamond, suspecting a game, leapt and barked around her legs. Then Hamish was standing before Alexandra, his hand on her arm. He was wearing only pyjama bottoms. His torso was bare, fluffy with blond hair. His shoulders were broader than Ned's. Perhaps, unlike Ned – at least with Alexandra – Hamish favoured the missionary position, thus strengthening the forearms.

'Just let Jenny go,' said Hamish. 'She's very upset. The whole thing must have been traumatic. And no understanding at all from you, which is what the poor woman needs. You're behaving very badly towards her: in your situation it's not wise.'

'What situation and what about what I need?' asked Alexandra. 'It's hard for women when their married lovers die,' said Hamish, piously. 'Rightly or wrongly, the widow has the sympathy of the world: surely you could afford to spare a little for her?'

16

Everyone who was anyone called that morning, by phone or in person.

Three people got through from the theatre: one to say Daisy Longriff was wonderful, Alexandra shouldn't worry; two others to say Daisy Longriff was perfectly dreadful, Alexandra shouldn't worry. She mustn't come back to work until she was beginning to mend. They were all thinking of her. There was no matinee on Monday, so most would come down to the funeral. But perhaps there'd be a memorial service in London later?

The postman came to the door and wept a little and said he missed Ned's smiling face. He was a thin young man with cropped red hair and a little red moustache. He usually called before eight and Ned seldom smiled before ten, and least of all did Ned ever smile at the postman, whom he suspected of dropping letters behind hedges if it didn't suit him to deliver them. But forget that; think the best. Alexandra made the postman a cup of tea. He asked for more sugar than she provided. He said if Ned's shoes were going spare he could do with them. Alexandra picked a pair out of the cupboard and handed them over. It was true they were expensive shoes and nearly new: but she had to be practical, as did the postman. Not that the postman did much walking: he had a van.

The postman sat in Ned's chair and took off his own shoes, which were indeed battered, and put on Ned's. They fitted well. Then he asked Alexandra where the bin was and threw his old shoes in it. He went away in Ned's shoes, pleased as Punch, having won some kind of final victory. Diamond growled, but did not bite.

The *Mail*, the *Express* and the *Telegraph* called to say they didn't want to intrude into private grief, at which Alexandra put down the phone.

The *Sun* called to say they wanted to send flowers to the funeral, when was it? 'Such a fine critic, such a loss to the theatrical profession.' Alexandra laughed before she put down the phone.

Dr Moebius left a message to ask Alexandra to call to see him, and please could she put Mrs Linden in touch: Mrs Linden wasn't answering her phone.

Sheldon Smythe called for Hamish. Hamish took the call in the other room. I'm the wife, thought Alexandra; he's only the brother. But it seemed men liked to deal with men.

The postman who took Ned's shoes had left letters: coloured square envelopes, handwritten, instead of the long white ones which usually came. Alexandra glanced through a few of them, letters and cards of condolence. How wonderful Ned was, how charismatic; their hearts went out to Alexandra. They meant it, too. She was grateful, even while beginning to consider their judgements faulty. But then she herself was apparently without judgement and noticed nothing, so what had she to complain about? Insensitive to atmosphere.

The Romanoff of the Golf Course. Ned had never described Irene thus in Alexandra's hearing. She would have laughed if he had. Would Jenny Linden have the wit to make up such an epithet? It seemed unlikely. But she could have got it from Abbie, or Vilna, or anyone, who got it from Ned. It sounded like Ned. He'd just never said it to her.

'Marmalade'; a gift from Ned? No. Most likely simple chance: lots of orange cats in the world. And Ned, perhaps, on some innocent professional encounter with Jenny Linden, had happened to say, 'My wife's mother has a cat just like that,' thus enabling Jenny Linden to concoct her story.

Oh, clutching at straws!

17

Theresa called and dusted round a bit, crying. She didn't like doing housework, feeling she was employed to look after Sascha, but was always prepared to help out in an emergency.

Hamish came out of the study and asked Theresa to clear out the utility room, and put the dog's blanket through the machine; so Theresa sulked and told Alexandra she could stay only till midday. Alexandra told Theresa that Hamish was from Scotland and was used to telling people what to do, Theresa was not to take it badly.
'He talked to me as if I was a servant,' complained Theresa, but agreed to stay: she could do all the house except the utility room.

Alexandra herself put the blanket through the machine. Hamish was right. The blanket was thick with dog hair, and smelt of warm wet dog even when Diamond wasn't in his basket. Diamond growled at Alexandra when she took the blanket away. Diamond was becoming more and more disaffected. He missed his routine, he missed Sascha, he missed Ned. Alexandra found herself mistrusting and almost disliking Diamond. The fact was, in going for walks with Jenny Linden, Diamond had betrayed her. Perhaps Alexandra wouldn't keep Diamond, in spite of the fact that everyone obviously expected her to? Perhaps she would give him away? What sort of guard-dog was he, anyway, who wouldn't bark at a knock at half past seven in the morning, but sleep until he was called? By Jenny Linden.
In the bottom of Diamond's basket Alexandra found a chewed plastic bracelet – bright red. Not her own. Diamond cringed

and looked guilty. Alexandra lifted the bracelet out and called Theresa and asked if it was hers. Theresa said it wasn't hers though Alexandra was pretty sure it was. But why should Theresa lie?

Diamond took the bracelet under discussion in his mouth and went upstairs and stood outside the closed door of the master bedroom, and when Alexandra opened it went inside and laid the bracelet on the brass bed and stood with his head bowed in shame. It was Diamond's habit thus to return chewed objects to the place of taking, when his misdemeanours were found out. Of course Diamond might have got it wrong, this time. Who was to say a dog had a perfect memory? Like humans, presumably they could get muddled.

Alexandra aimed a kick at Diamond: she couldn't help it. Diamond yelped. Alexandra was instantly sorry and guilty. Diamond returned and licked her hand and growled. 'Diamond's guilt trip,' she and Ned would say. Diamond's self-humbling made Alexandra squirm and Ned laugh. Ned laughed a lot.
'It isn't mine, honestly,' said Theresa. 'Honestly. Cheap old thing. It might be Mrs Linden's, from the look of it.'
It didn't seem in the least Jenny Linden's style, though, not at all. And the 'honestly' seemed wrong.
'I expect Mrs Linden came here often,' said Alexandra, as casually as she could. 'When I was away? She helped Mr Ludd quite a lot with his work.'
Theresa was not deceived. All Alexandra did was to humiliate herself.
'She'd come to work with Mr Ludd sometimes,' said Theresa. 'They did those books together. But there wasn't anything in it. I wouldn't want you to think there was.'
'I should think there wasn't!' said Alexandra. 'Good Lord!'
'He loved you so much,' said Theresa, bursting into more tears: she was unrestrained in her weeping. 'And you loved him, and now he's gone. That poor little innocent boy, orphaned! It makes you think!'
'It does indeed,' said Alexandra, and left Theresa to weep alone.

Even her tears seemed on a larger scale than the rest of humanity's.

Hamish came out of the study and put his long thin arms round Theresa's bulk to comfort her. She lay her giant's head upon his shoulder, in trust. Ned would never have done that.

Of course guests sometimes used the master bedroom to leave their coats, at parties. The bracelet might have been pulled off with someone's sleeve. Yes, that was it. Most things had a harmless explanation. The whole world, including Jenny Linden, could believe Ned was having an affair with Jenny Linden, and be wrong. Just as the whole world could believe she and Eric Stenstrom were having an affair, and be wrong.

Lately Alexandra had come to see her mind as a computer. It searched for distant and improbable connections. It took its time: what it was doing was difficult. There were not enough megabytes installed. The egg-timer that meant 'wait, wait, I'm searching, I've got a problem', was nearly always up on screen these days, thwarting her.

Alexandra found that lately she'd blinked more than usual. The thoughts and ideas that came to her no longer drifted vaguely and easily here and there: each one had to be caught, translated into words, registered. Each registering was indicated by a blink. Information, blink. But she had to use some kind of mind keyboard to type in problems and propositions. Hours, even days later, conclusions were reached. One came to her now.

'How did Ned come to think I had some kind of sexual relationship going with Eric Stenstrom?' Why, because Jenny Linden put it into his head that it was so. 'Why did Ned not confront me with this?' Because it suited him not to: because he was proud and would not lower himself to enquire. 'Would I have taken the part of Nora opposite Eric Stenstrom's Torvald if I thought for one minute Ned believed we had had, were having, or ever would have an affair?' No. 'If Ned believed I was betraying him with Eric Stenstrom, would he have fucked the next woman who practically lay down in front of him with her legs open?' Yes. Probably.

She switched the computer off. Breathed. Rested. Switched it on again.

Click, click, the computer went. It made the occasional little bleep. Hard disc in place. Mouse found. Even as Alexandra thought this – and how laboured the thoughts still were: one thing after another, plodding and careful – a real mouse, little, brown and quick, ran out from a cupboard in front of her, out of the kitchen door to where Theresa was blubbing and cleaning out the grate in the living room. The mouse seemed to exist as a demonstration of the way the spirit always tends to become flesh; the way a psychological phenomenon offers itself up in concrete form: the way verbal puns offer themselves for literal interpretation.

The quick and the dead. She was quick and Ned was dead. The egg-timer had vanished. She felt she could just about catch up, match event to word, word to thought, thought to conclusion, and conclusion to action. Theresa saw the mouse, let out a yell, straightened up, banged her head, shook the ammonite off the shelf, and it split. Not perfect any more.

18

During the morning Abbie called on Vilna. Abbie and Arthur had been asked to a Hunt Ball and Abbie needed something to wear. Vilna had said she'd be glad to lend Abbie something from her own extensive wardrobe, and how did it happen that she, Vilna, had not been asked to the Hunt Ball? Was it perhaps because her husband was in prison? Or because she couldn't help talking about the poor little foxes? Abbie said it was more likely to be the latter.

Abbie stripped down to her sensible white bra and pants, and her non-ladder knee-highs, and stood by Vilna's built-in cupboards while Vilna handed her garment after garment and Abbie shook her head. Too tight, too bright, not her, whatever.

'I am the one who should be miserable, not you,' said Vilna. 'I am generosity itself. These people come to my dinner parties and eat venison off plates which cost £250 each and drink the best champagne out of Venetian goblets, and they are happy enough to do that; it is all take, take, take, and not give, give, give. They do not know how to behave. They do not invite me in return. Well, I forgive them. I am like that.'
Abbie said she, Abbie, was not particularly like that. She was having a hard time forgiving Alexandra. At first she, Abbie, hadn't believed Jenny Linden when she said Alexandra was having an affair with Eric Stenstrom. She thought Jenny was looking for excuses because of her relationship with Ned.
'Why should a woman in love need excuses?' asked Vilna. 'If she loves, she fucks.'
Abbie sighed. Vilna's mother Maria pottered around the room,

dressed in peasant black, with wrinkled grey stockings and wide flat brown shoes. She was making sure her daughter gave nothing valuable away to her treacherous friends. Maria fingered the gold tassels on the curtain's ropes, pretending to be protecting the furniture from the danger of fading in the sun's glare. She tutted and sighed and clicked with her false teeth. Vilna ignored her. Abbie had learned to do the same.

But if Alexandra had been having an affair with Eric Stenstrom all along, Abbie's work had been wasted, her sympathy misplaced, complained Abbie.

'I lugged that body about,' said Abbie, 'laundered those disgusting sheets – everything was all over them, everything – I got the doctor, got the ambulance, got Jenny out of there before Alexandra came; I kept Alexandra company, upset Arthur by staying away; and then Alexandra can't even tell me the truth, can't even be honest with me, so I feel like a fool when even that ass Hamish seems to know more than I do. What's he doing, poking around in all those private papers? Alexandra is so hypocritical! Eric Stenstrom all this time. Poor Ned. No wonder he had a heart attack. Alexandra is the real murderer, not Jenny at all.'

'Eric Stenstrom,' pondered Vilna. 'What a dreamboat!' Much of Vilna's English, as Abbie observed to Arthur, came from old Hollywood films.

'What does Alexandra have that I do not?' And Vilna pulled in her flat, well-exercised belly yet further, thrust out her silicone breasts (Alexandra swore) and smiled her big white teeth into the mirror. 'Pot-bellied; dull little English face; though I must say her bosom isn't bad, as everyone knows; and now Eric Stenstrom on top of that. And Alexandra will inherit the house and those dull bits of furniture everyone talks about, and not have to put up with Ned. I said yes to Ned once but he couldn't get it up. No woman can put up with that.'

'I don't believe you, Vilna,' said Abbie. 'I just don't. Because you want a thing to have happened doesn't mean it has. And don't be too sure Alexandra will inherit the house.'

'Why should she not?'

'There may be debts to be paid,' said Abbie. 'Who knows? She doesn't have much head for business. She doesn't notice much. Is there anything just plain navy blue? I like navy blue.'

'Dreadfully dull on its own, darling,' said Vilna. 'Navy needs white and gold to amount to anything at all.'

'Alexandra practically threw us out yesterday,' Abbie complained. 'If she goes on like this she'll find herself with nobody.' Abbie decided that the gold braid and crimson tassel could be removed from a plain navy silk with a high collar and that would do well enough for a Hunt Ball with a lot of lesser gentry and prosperous farmers.

Maria left the room and Vilna took advantage of her absence. 'Darling,' said Vilna, 'there are no men round here, and now even Ned's gone and Clive's in prison, and I haven't for ages. What about you and me –?' Her bony little hand stole round to squeeze Abbie's languid breast in its sensible bra.

'Don't you do that,' shrieked Abbie, pushing the hand away.

'Oh, you English,' said Vilna. 'How you narrow your lives! Arthur is a new man. He would not care even if he noticed.'

'He's my husband and I love him,' said Abbie. 'Thank you for the dress but don't you ever do anything like that again.'

Vilna shrugged. She did not seem particularly upset by Abbie's rejection of her advances.

'At least we English don't have civil wars all the time,' said Abbie, quite unnecessarily, 'and if you don't like it here why don't you go home?'

Abbie remembered to take the dress but slammed the door as she left, so that all the security alarms went off and the guard-dogs barked, straining at the ends of their chains. Vilna liked foxes but disliked dogs.

19

During that morning Eric Stenstrom himself called Alexandra. 'Alexandra,' he said in his throaty voice, 'my dear. How are you?'

'I'm OK,' she said. 'I suppose.'

'I hear all kinds of things are coming to light,' he said. 'Things do when people die. When AIDS took my Petrie people turned up at his funeral and told me things I would rather not know. I sympathise. But now Ned's dead, does it matter? He can do you no more wrong. That's what I felt like when Petrie died.'

'It seems to matter,' said Alexandra. 'A great deal. I am either who I thought I was, or not. In the end it is important to apportion blame. There must be a day of judgment. No court will do it now, so I must sort it out myself.'

'At least all Petrie left me was herpes,' said Eric. 'I'm not HIV positive. He spared me that. If I can forgive your husband, so can you. He complained about my tights when I was playing Oberon at the National. He said they were too small. What sort of theatrical criticism was that?'

'Ned's sort,' said Alexandra. 'And I am not talking about forgiveness. There is no such thing. It may seem easier to appease, or self-interest intervenes and one chooses to forget. Or time does it for you. But that's all. Eric, there is a rumour going round down here that I'm having an affair with you.'

'If only you were, darling,' said Eric. 'If only I was other, I'm sure we would be. And we did try once, don't you remember, for the sake of my career? It was before I met Petrie, and fell in love.'

'We were both drunk,' said Alexandra. 'Ned was away in Norway. Hollywood wanted us, as a team, for the remake of *Gone with the*

Wind. We were good together, they thought. Six years ago. What were we playing?'

'*A Midsummer Night's Dream,*' said Eric. 'You were Titania. This was our big Hollywood break.'

'We thought we'd be turned down,' said Alexandra, 'because the producer was insisting on a heterosexual cast. And the attempt failed anyway so there was nothing to report. And Hollywood melted away, as it always does. For me, that is, not you. But I would rather that occasion wasn't bandied about. You never mentioned it to anyone, did you?'

'What, mentioned my shame?' asked Eric Stenstrom. 'Why should I do a thing like that?'

'You did, didn't you!' said Alexandra.

'I tried once again with a woman,' said Eric, 'and it worked. I may have mentioned the earlier attempt to her. It would have seemed only fair. We were quite close for a time. But it was a long way back. I can't really remember.'

'Who was she?'

'Some little set designer. She made models. She wasn't powerful like you: not a strong woman. She looked kind and she looked female and she looked like she didn't matter. But when it came to it, it wasn't any fun. I couldn't face a straight future. I went back to Petrie.'

'What was her name?'

'I can't remember,' said Eric. 'It was years ago. But her name was next to yours in the address book.'

Alexandra put the phone down, and sat down herself on the carved settle, *circa* 1670, oak, some woodworm eradication necessary. Now Ned wasn't there to do it, she, Alexandra, would have to. She and he had been putting it off for long enough. She went out to the garden. The comfrey was out of control: it was rooting everywhere. Blackcurrants squelched on the bough, unpicked. Greenfly multiplied on the roses, blackfly on every yellow flower around. She wondered where she would scatter Ned's ashes. Presumably they would contain the minerals needed for organic life. They would be wasted in such a fertile place: somewhere more desert-like would be preferable. Vilna's front garden perhaps, where the walnut tree had been cut down, illegally, to make room for the guard-dog kennels; and lime from old dismantled walls had wrought havoc with the pH balance. That could do with a soupçon of Ned. In the meantime she would abandon all efforts to keep this lot in order. Vegetation was greenfly rampant: winter would come and the riot of vegetation all vanish anyway, except for a few browned, sodden plants which had the nerve to struggle on. She left the garden and went inside; but the house felt hostile. She supposed that to be Hamish's presence.

When Hamish came out of the study he was in a bad temper. He asked when lunch would be ready. Alexandra said she personally wasn't hungry but there was canned soup in the cupboard and bread in the breadbin. He asked her if she had finished the funeral list, and she said she had got to the T's. But not yet to the U's onward. Hamish said if they didn't go off today there was no point in sending them. He asked Alexandra to sign a cheque to Mr Lightfoot for £1,500; pointing out that since the number of guests did not affect the bill it was a waste not to have as many as possible.
'A very Scottish way of looking at things,' said Alexandra, and Hamish berated her for such a stereotypical and Anglocentric response. She said she had meant the remark, which was casual, in the sense of 'an endearing Scottish way' and that there had been nothing pejorative about it.

Hamish then moved away from the consideration of Alexandra's idleness to the matter of her negligence. Why had she not persuaded Ned to go to a proper doctor? Alexandra replied that Ned hated doctors. It must have been obvious to everyone, said Hamish, that Ned was ill, that his heart was damaged. Alexandra said it was not obvious to anyone. Hamish observed that at least Jenny Linden had cared enough to persuade Ned to go to a faith healer: so someone must have known he wasn't well.
'This is the first I've heard of it,' said Alexandra, and asked if it was Hamish's habit to consult with Jenny Linden rather than

with her. Hamish said he found Alexandra's attitude truculent and Alexandra said no doubt that was projection.

Thus her rare rows with Ned had run, until one or other of them laughed, when the curse was lifted. Now she laughed but Hamish didn't. He said he was glad she thought it was funny. The £1,500 would clear out her joint account with Ned; things were in a perilous state. Hamish remarked that it was as reasonable for himself to be in touch with Jenny Linden, as for Alexandra to be in touch with Eric Stenstrom. He revealed that he had picked up the extension and overheard the conversation. 'Then it will be apparent that Eric Stenstrom is gay,' said Alexandra, 'as Ned was well aware, so you can stuff all this rubbish.' 'I put down the receiver at once,' said Hamish. 'I do not listen in to obviously personal calls, and Ned in his letter referred to Stenstrom as a bisexual. As a consequence, Ned was understandably worried for your health, and his. It must have contributed to the strain and distress he endured.'

Alexandra asked if she could see this famous letter, and Hamish said no, in the light of her aggressive and unhelpful attitude he would not show it to her.
Alexandra asked Hamish if he could at least tell her the date of the letter: was it before the beginning of the *Doll's House* run? Hamish said yes. Alexandra asked how many years before. One year, five, ten?
Hamish said five. Perhaps.
Alexandra remarked that Ned, like everyone else in the theatre world, knew that Eric Stenstrom was single-mindedly gay, and probably HIV positive, though he denied it.
Hamish said gay was a false and confining definition: most gays, especially in the theatre world, were indeed bisexual, or so he understood.
Alexandra said anyway Ned would hardly have gone on having sex with a wife whom he suspected of having an affair with a gay – or bisexual, who cared? – who was HIV positive and admitted to having herpes, now would he?
Hamish said but he understood from Jenny Linden that she,

Alexandra, hadn't slept with Ned since the child was born. Alexandra said that may be what Jenny Linden wanted to believe but it was far from being the case.

'You mean Ned deliberately deceived Jenny Linden?' asked Hamish. 'Though I imagine it's what men do tend to say in such circumstances.'

'Try to understand,' said Alexandra, 'that Jenny Linden simply makes things up.' Hamish suddenly collapsed and started to cry for no apparent reason. It was as if he were a well which filled up with antagonism and when it was emptied that was that. He had to wait till it filled up again. Alexandra consoled him. It seemed required of her. He laid his head upon her shoulder, little-boy-like.

'It's the shock,' he said. 'I've lost my brother,' he said. 'Ned was all the family I had left.'

'You have me,' said Alexandra through her teeth. But Hamish's arms grew tighter round her, and for a moment again she thought it was Ned back: there was the familiar shock of intent which went with the touch, the sense of inevitability, the sheer meantedness, but this was Hamish, not Ned. It was nothing: what she'd felt was just a kind of earthquake aftershock, the shadow of the old moon in the new moon's arms; not the real thing at all.

'Don't,' she said. 'Don't!' and drew away.

'But if you were never faithful to Ned,' Hamish said. He grabbed her arm and pulled her towards him. He was the reverse side of Ned: the other side of a coin. Not very adult, not very male, not very nice. He pawed and picked at her; he didn't assault her or engulf her. He was a fly crawling over the skin, not a wasp stinging. 'Why are you being so fussy now? Haven't we had enough of this grieving widow act? Is there something the matter with me? Do you want to be fucked by film stars, is that it? Got used to better than me? Aren't I good enough?'

Now she was pushing him away, having to, her hand on his chest, and his face crumpled again.

'Everything's gone wrong in my life,' he mourned, 'everything. I want to go home. I hate this place. You have to forgive me. I don't know what I'm doing. I just wanted to be Ned, just for a moment. To be with you, to bring him back.'

'Ned's dead,' she said. 'How it rhymes. How it fits.'

'You'd better be nice to me,' he said. 'You'd better. Or else.'

He was like a child, back when Ned was twelve and he was ten. She ignored him. He went back into the study to sit among the piles of paper, once tidily confined, now scattered everywhere, in an order she suddenly saw might well not be rational.

Alexandra went down to the mortuary and sat by Ned's body.

'Did you or didn't you?' she asked him. 'Why did you take me to Jenny Linden's? I remember it so clearly: the kind of thing you would normally forget. Framed in my mind. She was a little flustered. She opened a bottle of wine. She said in her soft voice, "Well, might as well open this, I suppose." It was Barolo, I remember that. I wondered how she could afford it. Well, Ned? Well?'

Ned was there, but somewhere else. Off on his journey through the forest, expiating the sins he had committed. She understood it now. Of course Ned hadn't looked back. She wondered if Sascha would grow up to be like his father. That was the worst of it. If you hated the father, how did you not hate the child? When she touched his arm, she found it yet more compacted: the body seemed to radiate cold, to push her away. Ned was a metaphor turning to marble.

Mr Lightfoot came in to say Mr Ludd was to have company: a Miss Partridge, a seventy-five-year-old spinster, would be resting here for a day or so while the necessary decisions were made. He laid a hand on Alexandra's arm. Since Ned had died, all kinds of people had touched her. They were being kind, but diminishing her in their minds to child status.

'Forgive and forget,' Mr Lightfoot said to Alexandra. 'That's the motto!'

'I won't,' she said. 'This way I don't let him die. If there's no forgiving, there's no forgetting.'

20

Alexandra called her mother. Was Sascha all right? She hadn't seen him since last Saturday. Now she was worrying dreadfully. She missed him. Should she drive down tomorrow to visit?

'It's not sensible,' said Irene. 'You sound too upset. Sascha's perfectly happy playing with the kittens. Four marmalade, one white, and three tabby. He protects them from the father, who is a grotty tabby tom and wants to eat them.'

'But I'm getting anxious about him; I just need to be with him. Can I speak to him, please?'

'You've probably been ill-wishing the poor child,' said Irene. 'Undue anxiety in regard to a child is often a projection of the mother's own destructive impulses, and I quote.'

'Oh, God, Mother,' said Alexandra. 'What have you been reading?'

'A book,' said Irene. '*Mother: Friend or Foe?* It's very interesting. I'm not sure you're the best person to be his mother. But I take it with a pinch of salt. I know you must be feeling bad about Ned and that dreadful woman, and Sascha is so very like Ned. Same eyes, same chin. You might find yourself very hostile, unconsciously. Then accidents happen. I should leave him here a little longer. Perhaps not come down tomorrow. I don't want him upset. He is Ned's child, isn't he?'

'Mother!'

'Well, Eric Stenstrom isn't so unlike Ned to look at. Scandinavian eyes, strong chin, straight back. And it was all going on about the time you got pregnant with Sascha. I did rather wonder.'

'I can't believe you're saying this. How does Eric Stenstrom even come into it? He's gay. What is going on here?'

'It would explain why Ned started an affair with this woman. He

119

was humiliated. You playing opposite Eric every night for all the world to see. His Torvald to your Nora. All the critics could talk about was what a sexy production it was. In the scene when you dance the Tarantella: darling, when I saw it I practically had to avert my eyes, and I'm not easily shocked. I don't know how poor Ned was expected to react.'

'This is total insanity, Mother. The critics were beyond belief: even Ned laughed. The play isn't about sex, it's about female emancipation. Though you'd never have known it from reading the reviews.'

'You could have fooled a lot of us, darling,' said Irene.

'My dress slipped on the First Night and I finished the scene bare-breasted: it was that, or bring down the curtain, and for God's sake what did it matter? I had shoulder straps put on the costume and it was the first and last time it happened. Who cares?'

'It made your name, darling,' said Irene. 'I'm afraid very few thought it was an accident.'

'Mother, if you worry too much about what people think, you never get anything done. Ned would say that. And, please, how does it happen that now Eric Stenstrom's name is coming up? What do you think you know about me and him? Because there's nothing to know: ask him.'

'I kept quiet about it, darling, but that horrid little girl who played Mrs Linde – much too young for the part: why on earth was she cast? Someone's girlfriend, I suppose – what's her name?'

'Daisy Longriff,' said Alexandra.

'Daisy Longriff said at the First Night party that you and Eric were close. She said she would have been Nora and you Mrs Linde but Eric had it switched.'

'It was because I can act and she can't,' said Alexandra. 'There was nothing personal about it. But obviously she'd rather there was.'

'She told me you'd lost your costume on purpose. It was a publicity stunt, and planned.'

'I don't believe this,' said Alexandra. 'What a little bitch! Why did you listen to her? Do you have no loyalty to me at all? I always helped her all I could. I thought she liked me. At least no one will believe her. She's making a dreadful mess of Nora, I hear. That's something.'

'She does the Tarantella scene nude,' said Irene. 'The rest of the cast don't like it, but on the other hand they're taking bookings months ahead. Lexi, I really want to talk about Sascha's future. If she does it nude, you'll have to do it nude. Is this really what you want Sascha's future to be? Bad enough to have an actress for a mother, but a stripper! He is a Romanoff –'

'Jesus, Mother –'

'I know what you think about that; but it's true. The blood does flow. Ned would turn in his grave –'

'He's not in his grave yet, Mother. He's lying down there in the morgue, turning to marble, and all you can give me is this junk –'

She slammed the phone down. Picked it up, redialled.

'And if you think you're taking Sascha from me, Mother, you've got another think coming. I'm driving over to collect him tomorrow afternoon and that's that.'

'You mean poor little Sascha's to go to Ned's funeral? Just like that?'

Oh, icy mother; remembrance of things past.

'That's no problem,' said Alexandra. 'I'm not going to Ned's funeral. Ned doesn't deserve to have me there. If he can die in some slut's arms, that slut can do the burying. I won't.'

Silence.

'But you loved Ned.' Irene's voice had lost its ice. She was alarmed. 'He was your husband.'

'So what?' said Alexandra. 'So what? If he couldn't remember it, why should I?'

'There'll be a dreadful scandal, dear,' said her mother.

'The press will love it,' said Alexandra, bitterly. 'It will be good for bookings, and I will be blamed for that too.'

Alexandra put the phone down. She could hear Hamish heating soup in the kitchen. Friday today. Just the lawyer's meeting on Tuesday. Then Hamish would go. Thank God. Herself and Sascha alone in the house till the following Monday, settling down, getting used to lack of Ned. Theresa could come over on the Saturday, so Sascha felt easy with her after the three-week break. Then she, Alexandra, would stay up in London for the rest of the run; coming back for Sundays: Sascha would need to stay at The Cottage because of nursery school. It wasn't ideal, but it would have to do for now. The run would end in time; then she'd be back as a full-time mother; heaven knew when she'd work again.

Thank God for Theresa: natural, reliable, easy, kind. Ned would groan and say Theresa was more like an ox than a human being; was it good for Sascha to be so much in the company of an ox? Was it good for his brain cells? Would he lumber fatly through life? And Alexandra would say, OK, Theresa goes and you do full-time parenting, Ned, while I earn, and Ned would say, OK, OK, you win, Theresa stays. And both of them would laugh. Jenny Linden never made anyone laugh. She was too slow, too dull: her stolid flesh, the unlaughing, moist gap between her legs too eager, available and hungry to generate much mirth.

21

Alexandra remembered something. She called Abbie.

'Abbie,' said Alexandra, without preamble, 'what do you know about herpes?'

Abbie said she was in the middle of serving apple pie to her students. She couldn't talk now. She wasn't sure she wanted to, anyway. Perhaps Alexandra should call Vilna. Abbie's voice was cold.

Alexandra called Vilna, who said she was insulted to be asked such a question. Why did Alexandra think she should know anything at all about the subject? Because she was a filthy foreigner? Vilna was in a bad mood.

Alexandra went to see Dr Moebius, who by some miracle had a free appointment, and reminded him of a time five years back when she was tested for the herpes virus. Ned had developed a herpes pustule on his penis. He had become angry and bitter: in fact, as she could now see, Hamish-like. Ned had avoided sexual relations with her, Alexandra, for a week. He had blamed his infection on her. He claimed she had spoiled his life. She had been with another man; no matter how she denied it, Ned would not accept it. He was, he said, bitterly hurt, upset, betrayed. What other reason could there be? Since it was not him, it must be her. Alexandra said the virus could be dormant for years; neither of them had exactly been virgins on marriage. Ned said the chances of that were small. No, Alexandra had betrayed him. Alexandra wept and smarted. Went without Ned's knowledge to Dr Moebius for a test: lo, she had no such virus! Ned would not accept the verdict. Dr Moebius was a famous mis-diagnostician. Now the whole village would know their disgrace. Alexandra, too guilty, as she could now see, because of her secret scuffle with Eric Stenstrom to hold to her own opinion, was wholly wretched, but admitted to nothing. For five days the uproar lasted. Ned's single pustule went: with it, his alter ego departed. Thereafter he was Ned again; friendly, rational and kind. Life went on as usual. The incident had been forgotten, drifted off into the past. Now she replayed it to Dr Moebius, looking for explanation.

Dr Moebius looked at his watch. Could he perhaps refer Alexandra to a counsellor? Death should put all things in proportion. A herpes virus could not survive in a dead body. It needed warmth, and a way of getting out. Which it now didn't have. But he did have patients waiting, with current rather than past problems to discuss.

Alexandra asked if it wasn't more likely that Ned had been in close contact with someone who had just been in close and frequent contact with someone with a flagrant herpes infection, than that, having been dormant for years, the virus had reactivated itself. Of course, said Dr Moebius. And could she please ask Mrs Linden to be in touch.
'That bitch can rot in hell for all I care,' said Alexandra. Dr Moebius looked startled.
Alexandra left.

She could 'forgive' Ned for fucking Jenny Linden over the course of a year – a year in which she had been away a lot. Just. Jenny Linden the seductress; Ned lonely and jealous. But she could not forgive a sexual relationship which had been going on for some years; in which she, Alexandra, had been laughed at, manipulated, and insulted behind her back. No, she could not.

She went home.

22

Alexandra went up to her bedroom and stared at the bed. She pulled back the bedclothes and sheets and examined the mattress where it had troubled her shoulder. She thought, yes, a spring might well have broken. She got a pair of scissors and cut through the fabric and revealed the strange concoction of wadding and wires within, now bulging out like a hernia. It was like opening a body, like cutting skin: without the flawless restraining surface everything fell to pieces. Yes, a piece of wire had snapped. Now how had that happened? The strenuous efforts of Ned and Jenny Linden? She got the scissor blade beneath the fabric of the mattress and sheared it wherever she could. She found one broken spring, at buttock level.

Alexandra went out to the barn and brought back the axe with which Ned had split logs. Diamond followed her.

She went back upstairs again with the axe and began to chop away at the base of the bed; some wood, some of it metal. She stove it in, in its middle. Diamond, witness to the life, barked and barked. She aimed savage blows at the curlicued brass rods which composed the headboard; they at least buckled and broke. That was satisfactory. But for the most part the bed just stood there, defying her. The axe blade merely slipped and slid where it met the metal of the frame. She would be lucky to avoid hacking herself by mistake. She didn't care. Destruction was harder than she thought. But at least the bed was now unusable. The mattress beyond repair.

Hamish was trying to restrain her arm. She whirled on him, axe held high. Then she dropped her arm, dropped the axe.

'Are you on drugs?' he asked.

She had to laugh. She went through the house finding everything of Ned's she could: raincoats from the hall, binoculars, Wellington boots, the guitar left over from his hippie days, T-shirt from the 'Save the Roman Cemetery' campaign, his entire Ibsen collection, the CDs, the old 78s, the video tapes he liked and she did not and flung them into the bedroom. She carried up the stairs, on her own, the easy chair he favoured, far too heavy a task for anyone in a normal state of mind. She shoved that on top of the wrecked bed. She smashed the bathroom mirror because Ned had looked in it too often, and threw that in with the rest. She went to the linen cupboard and found the green sheets that Abbie had laundered, and tore them hem from hem with a little help from the scissors, and flung them in too. Then she locked the door and turned to see Dr Moebius facing her, Hamish behind him.

'Shall we calm down, Alexandra?' he said. 'I could have you sectioned.'

'I am perfectly calm,' said Alexandra. 'And please call me by my proper name: Mrs Ludd.'

He was taking notes. She could see she should be careful. She was a widow with a child; a woman without a husband to give her authenticity. She was an actress, which suggested promiscuity and profligacy. If Social Services got involved she could end up with Sascha in care, at best with her mother, at worst with abusing foster parents. She was vulnerable. Society now required from her as a mother emotional correctness: she must subdue anger; she must practise understanding and forgiveness. She had better go to the funeral – hand in hand with Jenny Linden, if required. She smiled at Dr Moebius.

'On second thoughts,' she said, 'do by all means call me Alexandra. I know you're here to help me. And you're right, I need help.' A show of gratitude always went down well, when dealing with authority.

It appeared that Hamish had called Dr Moebius. After all, she had been running wild with an axe, a danger to herself and others.

'I'm so sorry if I alarmed you, Hamish,' said Alexandra. 'I was just trying to move the bed: I thought I'd give Sascha the bigger bedroom. Then the brass bed turned out to be too wide to get through the door. I wanted it in bits the better to reassemble it, that's all. As for the rest, I'm just getting Ned's things in one place for sorting. Oxfam will be round any moment. There's a lot here can be recycled.'

Dr Moebius was smiling now, and nodding. Even Hamish seemed pacified. It was easy, once you understood what was going on.

'I'm seeing Jenny Linden this evening,' she told Dr Moebius, easily. 'Poor thing, she's had such a hard time. I'll try and persuade her to get round to see you. She and I really must be friends. We have so many memories to share. We can help one another through this hard time: make the journey through grief together. Perhaps we should give her a lift to the funeral, Hamish?'

'That would be generous of you, Alexandra,' said Hamish, though he looked at her a little suspiciously.

'I thought perhaps it would be best if little Sascha doesn't come to the funeral,' Alexandra appealed to Dr Moebius. 'But what do you think?'

'Seven is the lowest age we recommend for funerals,' said Dr Moebius. 'You're right. Keep him away. Divert him. Then take the little chap aside, talk him through what happened. A mother's instinct is often best. He'll need extra mothering now. What we used to call TLC. Tender loving care.'

'What do we call it now?' Alexandra asked, without thinking, but heard tendentiousness in her own voice and quickly continued, 'I have some borage in the garden. Shall I make tea? You know the Ancient Greeks drank borage in times of bereavement? Borage is the solace for grief.'

'So where is the child now?' asked Dr Moebius, sipping his tea, which was not, as it turned out, unpleasant if taken with enough organic honey, though heaven knew how control was exercised over the bees so they supplied only the relevant purest nectar. His notebook was still out, but at least closed. 'I see no sign of him around. Is he asleep? Through all the furore?'

'He's with my mother,' said Alexandra. 'I'll be driving over to see him tomorrow. I do miss him so much! I'm making his new room ready for him. I thought if the house changed in little respects, the major respect – his father not there any more – wouldn't be so horrendous for him.'

'Very wise,' said Dr Moebius. 'But I do think perhaps you should see a grief counsellor.'

'I know a good one in Bristol,' said Alexandra. 'Leah someone or other.'

'Leah?' said Dr Moebius. 'Does she do grief as well? Well, I'm glad. She's very good.'

23

Alexandra could see the wisdom of doing what she was told. She felt an agreeable sense of cunning: what she imagined a vixen would feel, midwinter, hungry, desperate but so full of plans she'd scarcely notice, staring through a hedge as a frosty dusk fell, and the silly hens were locked away by a slow man in Wellington boots, footfalls crackling on already icy grass; and lo, there was a new rat-hole in the side of the henhouse, and the she-fox could see it, and the man plodded back to the house – and now the moon and the night-hour gave permission –

Alexandra looked up Leah's number in Jenny Linden's address book and called it up. She sat on the settle at the foot of the stairs, where she could see the back door, so often used, and the front door, so seldom used, and thought Ned would come in through the back any minute, but he didn't.

She could hear Hamish moving about in the study. What was he doing? He paced a lot, and wept a little judging by the state of his eyes. She could see that to lose a sibling was hard: it could only seem unnatural: out of time, out of order, a vicious rerun of your own departure into nothingness. Widowhood was a normal state. Most married women endured it, unless divorce intervened. Perhaps that was the merit of divorce.

'Hello,' said Leah, in her soft, ingratiating voice, with its hint of reproach. 'How can I help you?'

Alexandra imagined Leah, on no good grounds, to be a thin version of Jenny Linden: colourless hair falling limply and simply, *au naturel.* Leah would not have Jenny Linden's stubborn, sexy helplessness in the face of her own passions, which men found so attractive. She employed some other, even greater power over others: she could murmur 'worst fears' over the telephone and practically kill you. After that you would get better: turn the curse into a blessing but no thanks to her.

'I am Alexandra Ludd,' she said.

'I was expecting to hear from you,' said Leah.

'Why's that?'

'Jenny has told me how distressed you are,' said Leah. 'I imagined you would soon seek help.'

'Why should I choose you,' asked Alexandra, 'of all people?'

'You already have,' said Leah. 'You've been seeking to incorporate everything that's Jenny: stealing her writings, speaking to me with her voice.'

Jesus, thought Alexandra, these people interpret even attack as dependency. Give them a situation, they'll twist it any old how to come out on top.

'But you'll deny my interpretation,' said Leah, who appeared to be able to read minds, even over the phone. 'That too is natural. And don't be surprised by the degree of your distress. The poorer the relationship to the deceased, the harder it is to move through the grieving process.'

'You're telling me this for nothing?' asked Alexandra. 'Shouldn't I be paying? I bet this wisdom doesn't come cheap, either.'

'Ned paid three sessions in advance,' said Leah. 'If you want to step into his shoes, by all means do so. I loved him: I love all my clients. When one goes, it is as if a member of my own family goes.'

'Bully for you,' said Alexandra. 'Actually the postman's in his shoes. Ned's only got bare feet. His toes are quite, quite blue, and stiff, though shrinking. He has almost perfect feet: very straight toes. His mother, in spite of being Scottish, always made sure his shoes fitted.'

There was a short silence.

'I don't quite follow you,' said Leah.

'I shouldn't think you would,' said Alexandra, confident in her own superior wit, her fox-like mastery of the situation.

'You put too much faith in the intellect, Mrs Ludd,' said Leah, sharply. 'Ned always said so. Sometimes it is better to put cleverness aside, and let the feelings flow.'

'I'll do my best,' said Alexandra. 'Thank you for the advice.'

'I'm glad you've come to me for help,' said Leah. 'And I'm so glad you speak of Ned in the present tense. He is alive and well in you, as he is in Jenny.'

'Yes, isn't that nice,' said Alexandra.

'Jenny is doing very well, by the way. She is moving swiftly. I have been able to pass her on to the angry phase.'

'I'd noticed,' said Alexandra. 'So you reckon I should come and see you?'

'I'm very booked up,' said Leah. 'I don't normally do telephone work, but I can see this consultation is useful to you.'

'I hadn't realised it was a consultation,' said Alexandra. 'I thought it was a conversation.'

'Oh no,' said Leah, firmly.

'Well, perhaps I could take Ned's next appointment,' said Alexandra, 'since he won't be turning up.' Diamond crouched at her feet, head on her lap, looking doleful. Jenny Linden had not been round to take him for his walk, or perhaps he wanted food, or missed Sascha. Or even, of course, Ned. Perhaps Diamond should go down, like everyone else, to view the body. But the cold in the morgue would get to his bones. It wouldn't be fair.

'He and Jenny would come for an appointment together on Tuesdays at eleven,' said Leah.

'That's nice,' said Alexandra: the rat-hole wasn't as big as she thought. She was wedged.

'We would talk quite often about the possibility of Ned's getting together with you again,' said Leah, with a hint of apology, but the merest hint.

'How good of you,' said Alexandra. She could see the hens; she couldn't get at them. She snapped and snarled. They squawked.

'But your worlds had become so very different,' said Leah. 'You had grown apart. Ned was a very spiritual man. I don't think you realised. Do reconsider your choice not to attend with Jenny.

Reconciliation is so important; you should join together in love for Ned.'

'I'm sure you're right,' said Alexandra. 'But I still don't think I'll take up the offer.' She withdrew from the rat-hole, to reconsider her position.

'Of course, what Ned had to say to me in our sessions together must remain confidential,' said Leah. 'Those are the ethics of my profession.'

'You must send me a copy some time,' said Alexandra. She would gnaw away at its edges, enlarge the hole. 'But perhaps you could see this as a joint consultation, Ned and me, his and hers, his spirit here in principle. His fucking ghost's been banging round the house. I could probably still bring him along.'

'Ned's advance payments were for three individual sessions,' said Leah. 'I suppose I could count this as one and a half.'

'Yes, why not,' agreed Alexandra. 'Good idea!'

' "Ghost" is not a word we use,' said Leah. 'It has unfortunate connotations. We prefer to say "soul". And strong language doesn't upset me, if it helps you in some way, but I am sorry to say it does upset the telephone company. So please refrain. I take it the anti-love expletives are used freely in your theatrical world.'

'They do get bandied about a bit,' said Alexandra. 'And Ned himself wasn't averse to a shit, a fuck and a cunt.'

Wood was splintering in her mouth. She was aware that she was starving. If she didn't eat, she'd die. Cluck, cluck, cluck, went the silly hens.

'In your company, perhaps,' said Leah, 'but certainly never in mine, or Jenny's. It is probably some residual violence of expression lingering in the air which prevents his soul from settling, as you say is the case; evil making itself apparent in the material world.'

'Ah, that's it!' cried Alexandra. 'My fault again! It's the bad language does it!'

'Try to accept what I say, Alexandra,' said Leah. 'Denial can cause cancer. We take the poison back into ourselves. I believe your father died of cancer.'

'These hereditary problems are gender-linked,' said Alexandra, cunning again. The hole was big enough.

There was a short pause.

'And then of course,' said Leah, 'on top of the growing spiritual incompatibility, there were your and Ned's sexual difficulties.'

'Oh, what were those?'

'He felt you smothered him,' said Leah. 'And of course, as I unblocked his animus and it could flow freely, he looked for more anima in his partner.'

'You mean big tits?' asked Alexandra. 'Ned talked to you in this detail? To you, a stranger. About his and my sex life?' Her voice, she found, had risen a pitch. Her mouth was bleeding, her fox-teeth were broken. How would she tear the meat once she had it?

'I am his therapist,' said Leah primly. 'That's what therapists are for, surely? There is no shame.'

'But I don't know you!' cried Alexandra, before she could stop herself. Her pulse was beating faster; her heart was suddenly thudding. 'You are taking even this away from me.'

'I know sex was very important to you,' said Leah. 'Ned would complain to me that after you and he had sex you would be so happy.'

'Complain?' The man in the Wellington boots was plodding towards her. He had a gun. He raised it.

'It made him feel manipulated; as if sex was all you wanted him for. And you were so often away. You would come home just for that, for penetrative sex, not loving sex.'

Bang, bang in her head.

'You prurient old cow!' shouted Alexandra, so that Hamish came running from the study.

'I understand your anger,' said Leah.

'No one understands my anger,' shrieked Alexandra.

'This session is at an end,' said Leah. 'Worst fears!', and put the phone down, and the fox slunk away; wounded, howling. She would never recover.

'You mustn't upset yourself so,' said Hamish. Alexandra put Leah on hold until, as Leah would have said, she could deal with it.

24

That night, as Alexandra lay sleepless in Sascha's narrow bed, Hamish came into the room. He was wearing Ned's dressing gown and nothing beneath it. He had lighter body-hair than Ned's, and thinner, longer legs, but warm flesh, not marble. He offered comfort, there was no doubt about that: he was good-looking; some essence of Ned was there. The need to keep life going, to overlay death with sex, was strong. She lay still. He sat on the end of the bed. She moved her feet out of the way.

'Anthropologists tell us,' he said, 'that in many tribes when the husband dies the brother is expected to take over his role. I can't sleep. Can you?'

'Yes,' she said. 'If left alone.'

'I feel Ned everywhere. I think this is what he wants us to do: to comfort one another.'

'That may be wishful thinking, Hamish.' She sat up. She slept naked, as was her custom. She pulled the sheet up to cover her bosom. Gently, he pushed it down. She could not be bothered to resist. So, she had breasts. What woman didn't?

'I find your modesty the titchiest bit hypocritical,' said Hamish, amiably enough. 'Since your bosom is so easily bared to the millions.'

'About four hundred and twenty,' said Alexandra, angered, 'and not even a full house, since no one at that stage expected the show to be a success. But I don't mean to argue. Please go away.'

'You're going to need me,' said Hamish. 'More than you know. I think you'd just better give in and be nice to me.'

'Once you pay the Danegeld,' said Alexandra, 'you never get rid of the Dane,' and she avoided his hands, now on her breasts, and got out of bed. 'If I'm nice to you now you might never go away.'

She stood naked. She didn't care. Moonlight came through the window. She could see out to the garden, the privet hedge, the field. She wondered if Jenny Linden was out there, watching, trying to claim Ned's ghost as her own.
'You're quite insane,' Hamish said. 'You should have seen yourself with that axe. Totally out of control. I'm well out of it. Look at you! Exhibitionist, pure and complete. What Ned described as the Curse of Thespianism Descended. Actresses are sexually easy, he told me in one letter. Good at sex, but it's not important to them. Anyone will do. It's what they do for relaxation, between the only acts they care about. Actresses are not like real women at all. Make-believe females, with no centre, no soul, no capacity for real emotion.'
'Actors,' said Alexandra, and 'I don't believe in your letters. I've never seen them.' She was dressing. Pants, jeans, bra, T-shirt.
'I won't show them to you,' he said. 'They'd hurt you too much.'

She wondered where she was going to sleep. Abbie's? Vilna's? Both had seemed unfriendly. She needed sleep. She had to be fit to drive to her mother's the next day. With Sascha in the house Hamish would probably leave her alone. She doubted that he was dangerous. He would finger and upset; his instinct was to find a vulnerable spot and hurt as much as he could, but he wouldn't rape. He would not put himself so much in the wrong. No wonder Ned had kept him at a distance.

'Where are you going?' asked Hamish.
'To spend the night with Jenny Linden,' said Alexandra. 'You know what we Thespians are.'

25

Alexandra drove round to Jenny Linden's house. She found a parking space just outside and reversed into it, bumping Jenny Linden's car out of the way to do it. The sound of crunching metal brought people to their windows and doors, caused babies to cry, and bedroom lights to go on. Only in Jenny Linden's house did everything stay dark and quiet. But Alexandra had seen a pale, frightened face appear momentarily at the top window, then disappear.

She banged again and again at the door, using the big, heavy knocker to advantage. It was iron, antique, mid-nineteenth-century, in the form of a fish. Alexandra realised it was just the same as the one on her own front door. But that door was large and solid: this door was small and flimsy, and rattled and shook with every blow. Compete with Alexandra as she might, Jenny Linden would never get it right. Neighbours peered all down the street to see what was going on. It was past midnight.

It was not Jenny Linden who opened the door but her husband, Dave, in striped pyjamas and dressing gown. Alexandra remembered him from Kimmeridge.
'Go away,' he said. 'You're disturbing the peace. I will not have Jenny upset. You're persecuting her. I shall call the police.'
Jenny Linden appeared at his elbow, wearing a discreet pale blue nightie, its hem showing beneath a woollen dressing gown in dusky pink.
'Don't be too hard on her, Dave,' said Jenny Linden in her sweet little voice, her restraining hand on Dave's arm. 'Poor

Alexandra, she's having a hard time. She won't give herself permission to grieve.'

'You're too good to her,' said Dave. 'You're not fit to be out on your own.'

'Oh dear!' said Jenny Linden, peering out into the night. 'Someone's gone into the back of my car. Does that mean they have to pay, Dave?'

'Certainly does,' said Dave. 'You go back in and get your beauty sleep. I'll see to this.'

Jenny Linden nodded, smirked and went back in. Dave barred the door.

'How's the herpes, Jenny?' called Alexandra after her, loud and clear.

'Just get out of here before I call the police,' said Dave. 'You've done us enough mischief.'

'Me?' asked Alexandra, taken by surprise.

'So much the career girl, so eaten up with ambition,' said Dave, 'you couldn't even control your own husband.'

'I never thought it was a wife's role to do that,' said Alexandra. 'But I can see yours sees it differently. There's some new stuff called Zorimax. Very good for herpes, they say. Your wife caught it from Eric Stenstrom and passed it all round the neighbourhood.'

Dave seemed taken aback. She was glad it was not she who was, for once.

'Because if you two are getting back together again,' Alexandra said, 'it's the kind of thing a husband needs to know.'

'Jenny needs looking after,' said Dave, automatically, but his eyes had lost hers. He seemed bewildered.

'I thought Stenstrom was gay,' said Dave.

'Jenny proved otherwise,' said Alexandra.

'Bitch!' said Dave, and slammed the door in Alexandra's face. A sigh of response, a ripple of appreciation, went round the cluster of neighbours.

Alexandra pulled the iron knocker off the door – it was down to its last feeble nail-hold – someone's DIY job – and threw it in the gutter, untangled her car from Jenny's and drove all the way to her London flat. She could spend no more nights under the same roof as Hamish. She was exhilarated.

But soon Alexandra felt uneasy. What had she done? The best and safest place for Jenny Linden might well be in her husband's arms. Some people could get away with acts of malevolence; Alexandra never could. If she'd tugged someone's hair at school, a teacher would spot her. If she didn't pay a fare, she got caught. A policy of pleasant talking, optimistic outlook and an easy blindness to inconvenient fact had got her through life, or so she had thought, very well. She'd left it to Ned to be nasty, so she could be nice. Now Ned was dead and she, Alexandra, was left with the consequences of her own emotional idleness; she had encouraged Ned to be nasty to others and in the end he'd turned his nastiness on her. She had thought herself the famous, the beautiful, the bountiful Alexandra Ludd, immune from disasters which afflicted others, but of course she was not. She was like some charming villa in a hot climate, set in a ravishing and luxurious garden, built on stilts, and termites had been gnawing away at the stilts for years – termites from a whole assortment of nests: Resentment, Envy, Jealousy, Lust, Ambition, Malice, Spite (and the termites from Resentment have the strongest jaws, the most powerful bite of all) – and now see, the whole edifice was about to tumble into mud.

26

Ned and Alexandra's London *pied-à-terre*, 13 Angliss Street, was
to the north of Sloane Square, the top half of a small, quaint
house in a little street barred to traffic. There were two bedrooms, a small kitchen, a bathroom, a living room and a balcony.
The place was just about large enough for Ned, Alexandra and
Sascha, though if Theresa came too it was a squash. Theresa's
agreeably firm, white-skinned flesh came in contact with dressers
and porcelain, and blue and white china; she'd knock her big
head against the wall-lamps and bathroom fitments; the break-
ages were dreadful. Sascha clomped and jumped about in too
small a space for comfort and had to be hushed because of the
people living below – an old couple in their eighties, fortunately
deaf: they could not hear the noise but could watch flecks of
plaster dust falling from their ceiling when Sascha cried, 'Watch
me! Watch me!' and jumped from sofas or did his sudden if
ineffectual somersaults. He would fall sideways, not properly
head over heels. But the place was near enough Theatreland. At
a pinch, Alexandra could walk to matinees, and in the summer to
evening performances, before dark made the streets dangerous.

Here Ned and Chrissie had lived, before Ned met Alexandra
and they fell in love, and Ned and Chrissie parted. Divorced.
Then the house had been divided: Chrissie had sold her half
and gone to live with horses in Sussex. Ned kept his half as a
pied-à-terre for himself and Alexandra, buying The Cottage out
of money left him by his and Hamish's mother. Ned was convinced that London was no place to bring up a child – pollution
was bad and streets dangerous, and Sascha himself over-lively –
so one or the other of the parents would always take him back

to the green fields, the Virginia creeper and the roses of his real home after a day or so in the city.

Alexandra arrived at four in the morning. She was worn out. She had not eaten for days. But she must sleep now. She was too tired to eat. She went into her bedroom and turned on the light. There was someone sleeping in her bed. A woman. Alexandra turned off the light quickly, went into the second bedroom, lay down without undressing, and slept.

Alexandra did not wake till noon. She had a headache. She took some aspirin, had a shower and went into the kitchen. A woman she did not recognise was cooking spaghetti. She was in her forties, had short straight hair and an intelligent, reproachful face. Alexandra supposed she was some kind of academic. The woman acknowledged Alexandra's presence with a curt nod, but did not seem anxious for conversation. Alexandra put her dirty clothes into the washing machine, started the cycle, and only then said:
'Who are you?'
'Chrissie Ludd,' said the woman. 'And now Ned has died, this place is mine. I don't mind you staying until you sort yourself out, but don't make it too long. A couple of months will be fine.'
'I don't think that can be so,' said Alexandra. She feared a rerun of Jenny Linden. She, Alexandra, was the second wife, this one the first. They had never met. Ned had been at pains to keep the two women apart. He had described a neurasthenic, malicious woman, who drank too much and was forever on the edge of a breakdown. He, Ned, had married her out of pity, but eventually, after she had brought home a drunken teenager for a one-night stand, had decided he and she must part. But she had divorced him, eventually. He hadn't bothered to divorce her even after he had met and fallen in love with Alexandra. The one, the true, the only love in the face of which all other loves must falter. So Ned had said.

Chrissie now said, 'According to the divorce settlement, the property remained in my name, but he had the right to live in it until he died, after which it reverts to me. Now he's dead, so here I am.'

'That isn't fair,' said Alexandra. 'Why should a court do anything so silly?' It was all she could think of to say.

'It was twelve years back,' said Chrissie. 'Fault still entered into these things. Ned's behaviour had been such I got much the better deal. He howled and struggled and squirmed about everything: he hated to part with a penny. He was a monster; but I stuck to my guns and won. You must have known. You were with him at the time. Very much with him.'

'I didn't know,' said Alexandra.

'You must be a very unobservant person,' said Chrissie. 'Anyway, here I am. And you're on your way out, so I've won. If you hang about long enough, things come round; you win. I should have got a chunk of his inheritance too, from his mother, but he didn't disclose it to the court. Ned always played his cards close to his chest. But you'll know that.'

She was straining the spaghetti into her, Alexandra's, colander. She seemed so much at home Alexandra felt unable to challenge her.

'So, do you have another man ready to go?' asked Chrissie, as if pleasantly. 'You look the type.'

'Ned isn't even buried yet,' said Alexandra. 'Why did you divorce him? What were the grounds?'

'You,' said Chrissie. 'Adultery. He brought you back to our bed. It hurt, that. I don't forget it. I walked out there and then. Bed's still there, in the same place. Fits the alcove. Good mattress: not too hard, not too soft. Makes you feel rough, though, that kind of thing. Took me five years to recover. I slept in that bed last night, like a top. Yes, things come round.'

'I'm sorry,' said Alexandra, bleakly.

'Look at your looks, look at mine,' said Chrissie. 'What chance did I have?'

'Looks aren't important,' said Alexandra. 'They count for very little.'

'That's what the pretty ones always say,' said Chrissie, and

141

laughed: haw-haw-haw. She had a deep voice, a brusque manner. You could see her breeding dogs, winning at Cruft's, biting back emotion. Not Ned's type. No wonder. But what was Ned's type? Herself? Jenny Linden? Perhaps Ned liked only women he could despise? How would she manage to work without this apartment? She would go to a lawyer: this woman could just be trying it on. Ned would have told her, surely? 'You don't look too good,' said Chrissie. 'You theatrical types, quite flimsy when it comes to it. I didn't shed a tear when I heard Ned died. Danced a tarantella. But that's your role, isn't it? Throwing the tits around in public. I expect Ned liked that. Always a bit kinky.'

She was eating her spaghetti now, with Sascha's tomato sauce from the squeezy bottle. She didn't offer Alexandra any.

'I'll replace all this when you go,' she said, indicating the fridge, the cupboards. 'Give you the monetary equivalent, if you prefer.'

'That's OK,' said Alexandra. 'Help yourself.'

'And you're welcome to the little bedroom,' said Chrissie, generous in return. 'Come and go as you like, treat it like home for a couple of months. No more.'

'What about the furniture?' asked Alexandra. 'Even if what you say is so, it's the matrimonial property. Ned's and mine.'

'Most of it's Ned's and mine,' said Chrissie. 'Or mine. I brought it to the marriage. I started out with quite a bit of money, but Ned spent it. Sometimes I think when it was gone, I had to go too. That also hurt. Did you bring him any money?'

'A bit,' said Alexandra. It had been quite a lot but she didn't mean to tell Chrissie that. She was sorry she had brought grief even to such an uncouth woman as this. Perhaps she had not been so uncouth to begin with? Perhaps this was where Ned's rejection led one.

'I'll put your clothes through the dryer,' said Chrissie, kindly, 'when they're ready. Why didn't you have a washer-dryer? I would have. They take up so much less space. You've got messages on the answerphone. I've changed the message out. No point hanging about.'

One message was from Mr Quatrop, the estate agent in Eddon Gurney. His condolences to Mrs Ludd, he didn't want to disturb her at such a time, but there was a potential buyer for The Cottage, very keen; he thought she should know.

The second was from her agent, Harry Barney. Harry said Amblin's casting director was over from Los Angeles, wanted to see her on Monday, only had Monday in London, but that was the day of the funeral: he'd said no on Alexandra's behalf. Hoped she was OK. A little trouble at the theatre he had to talk to her about, but not to worry.

Alexandra punched out Mr Quatrop's number. Chrissie interjected.

'Go ahead by all means. I've had the phone put on itemised, so we can sort out costs later. No problem.'

Alexandra pointed out to Mr Quatrop that The Cottage was not for sale, so what was he talking about?

Mr Quatrop said that Mr Ludd had been in only a week ago, on the Saturday afternoon, talking about the possibility of putting the house on the market; of course it was too early for Mrs Ludd to give the matter proper consideration, he was sorry to have bothered her, but no one wanted to lose a good prospect for want of asking. Poor Mr Ludd. It made you think.

'Yes, makes you think,' agreed Alexandra. 'You're sure my husband wasn't just checking out property prices?'

'Let me put it like this,' said Mr Quatrop. 'One gets a nose for this kind of thing. I viewed Mr Ludd's enquiry as the first step on the critical path which leads to a major sale, this one involving three properties.'

And he told Alexandra that Mr Ludd had been toying with the idea of joining forces with Mrs Linden to buy Elder House, the language school. He'd gathered from a hint here and a gleam in the eye there they hoped to develop the property after purchase as a centre for theatrical design. Mrs Linden had to get to the stationer's before it closed, and had gone off, so it might well have been that he, Mr Quatrop, was the very last person to speak to Mr Ludd.

'Mrs Linden came in with my husband?' asked Alexandra, 'to discuss the possible sale of The Cottage and Mrs Linden's cottage and the possible purchase of Elder House with the proceeds?'

'That is so,' said Mr Quatrop. 'I hope I haven't upset you in any way?'

'No,' said Alexandra.

'I'll be closing for the funeral,' said Mr Quatrop, 'as a mark of respect. Many local traders are doing the same.'

'How very kind of them,' said Alexandra.

'If you make long-distance calls,' said Chrissie, 'you should try the Mercury network. It's cheaper.'

Alexandra called her agent at his home number, in Richmond. She thought it might steady her. She asked what the part under consideration was. Harry Barney said it was for the lead in a major drama feature, opposite Michael Douglas – high-budget, high-profile – the casting guy had been in the audience on the famous First Night, thought Ludd had star quality, wanted an English accent. But that was the way the cookie crumbled. The only person you couldn't stand up for an audition was your husband's corpse – Harry Barney coughed an apology.

'Sorry. Never could express myself in these matters. Too much emotion.'

'Harry, you loathed Ned.'

'Yes, in life. But not in death. He was one of us.'

'Why did you hate him?'

'Not as strong as that, sweetheart. I didn't take all that business too well.'

'What do you mean?'

'Ned pulled strings to get Longriff the *Doll's House* part. Everyone said it was going a bit far. Wife and girlfriend in the same production. I managed to get you Nora, but it was a struggle. She got it anyway, in the end. That's what I wanted to talk to you about.'

'Go slower, Harry. Ned and Daisy Longriff?'

'Well, yes. You knew, didn't you?'

'No. But everyone else did?'

'Jesus, I'm sorry. Alexandra, shall I come over?'

'No, I'm just fine, Harry.'

'It wasn't anything serious, Alexandra. Never was. It was you he loved. Just had a funny way of showing it. The girls simply lay down in front of him. Anything for a good review. Of course, like as not he wouldn't give it. That's what I really hold against him. If you're going to be corrupt, go the whole way. Half-measures only hurt. The sex was nothing. A man's a man, girl. That's why I chose to be gay. And for me it's a choice; I could give it up any time I wanted. Joke?'

'Joke, Harry.'

'That's my girl, that's my Ludd. Jesus, one day I might stop all this and settle down and marry you.'

'I'm flattered, Harry.'

'Ned's trouble was he was eaten up with envy. Couldn't write, couldn't act, couldn't direct. Just loved theatre. And you, you could stand on your head and do it all. Envy's a terrible thing.'

'I can see that it is, Harry. Got to go now.'

'I'll put your more personal things into the small bedroom, shall I, Alexandra? And such bits of furniture as I think aren't mine?'

Alexandra said if Chrissie didn't go at once, she was calling the police. She, Alexandra, wanted proper documentation, proper consultation with her legal advisers, before any decision whatso-ever could be made in relation to the property. She had her and Ned's child to think about. Would Chrissie now just go? And how had Chrissie got in in the first place, anyway?

Chrissie said she had a key, she'd always had a key, she'd dreamed for years of using the key again and now she had. Alexandra was a marriage-breaker, a bitch, a cow, a slag; she'd ruined Chrissie's life without a thought. Now it was her, Alex-andra's, turn.

But Chrissie went.

Alexandra waited for the locksmith to come and change the locks. Then she went to visit her mother.

27

Irene put Alexandra to bed in a nice bright attic room with eaves, its own television, a bathroom with fluffy pink towels and a view of the golf course. She gave her daughter buttered toast and Marmite, hot chocolate and two sleeping pills. Sascha plodded up the stairs and climbed in beside his mother. She held him in her arms and went to sleep.

She slept for fifteen hours until Sascha woke her by prising her eyes apart. He told her about the eight kittens. She told him Ned had died, gone to heaven, gone for a walk in a forest to look for God. Sascha asked if they could have one of the kittens. Alexandra said no, dogs didn't like kittens and kittens didn't like dogs. Sascha said yes they did. Couldn't they send Diamond to go for a walk with Ned in the forest and not come back like Ned? Alexandra said yes, that wasn't such a bad idea. She found she'd quite gone off Diamond.

Then she thought of Jenny Linden's marmalade cat and said she'd only have a kitten if it was a tabby. Sascha cried and stamped.

Alexandra looked at Sascha and thought he was very like Ned. Really he was a stranger to her. She found it difficult to believe they were intimately connected, in the way people said. The fact was, she seemed to have suddenly un-bonded with Sascha. She hadn't known that this was possible.

She presumed it would pass. It would have to. In the meantime she could act as she was trained to do. She would play loving mother.

'Poor little Sascha,' she said, 'but never mind. We'll see Daddy again in heaven.'

'I don't want to,' said Sascha. 'I want to stay here for ever, with Gran and the orange kittens.'

'But don't you want to go home and see The Cottage and Diamond and all your friends?'

'I don't have any friends,' said Sascha. 'They take my toys and you make me share and then they get broken.'

'There must be some grown-ups you like,' said Alexandra.

'I like Jenny,' said Sascha. 'She gives me toffees in the morning. You never do. She keeps them under the pillow especially for me. Oops.'

'Oops, what?'

'I wasn't to say. There's ghosts under the bed. They keep bumping in the night.'

Alexandra left Sascha doing somersaults on the bed, shrieking for joy in a way which would make social workers shiver, and crying, 'Watch me, watch me!' and went down to breakfast.

'I told him,' Alexandra said.

'How did he take it?' asked Irene. She wore a yellow tracksuit and had been out jogging. She was stirring honey into yoghurt. Her husband Abe, the banker, sat stolidly reading the *Telegraph*. They seemed a very happy couple.

'I'm not sure he took it in,' said Alexandra.

Sascha came down and said, 'Ned's gone for a walk in a forest and he isn't ever coming back, so I don't have to go home. I can stay here. I don't like Theresa. She's too big.'

He went out into the garden.

'There's no way,' said Abe, 'that Sascha can go home with you now, not in the state you are.'

'What sort of state is that?' asked Alexandra.

'Bad,' said Irene. 'Come back and collect him in a week, when you're ready. We're not trying to steal him from you.'

'I believe you,' said Alexandra. 'I think.'

She drove back to The Cottage. She liked driving. She turned on the radio and thought of nothing. Then she heard a programme called 'Theatre in London Today' and they were talking of Daisy Longriff's performance in *A Doll's House*. There was a discussion about art and nudity. Someone said it was like listening to *Hamlet* in Australian, and someone else said it was the most ravishing and intense performance he had ever seen. Someone said the theatre would be dark on Monday in remembrance of Ned Ludd, that Great Man of the Theatre, whose funeral was on that day: someone else said that was a rumour, to promote ticket sales. It was, they said, that Alexandra Ludd, probably the best serious female actor the country had, natural successor to Vanessa Redgrave *etcetera, etcetera,* was so prostrate with grief in their country home she might not be returning to the role. Well, thought Alexandra, now the bare-tits award goes to Daisy Longriff: I get to be serious. At last. But she didn't think much. She switched to another programme. It was easier.

28

Theresa lived with her family in Pig Cottage, a small stone house standing on its own at the highest point of the Drovers' Road, which led out of Eddon Gurney, over the hills to Selsdon, where there was a McDonald's and a library. In the past in these parts, Ned had told Alexandra, the shorter valley roads would become impassable in winter: mud, mire and flood water could make them dangerous. Then the shepherds would drive their flocks along the summits of the hills, and so the Drovers' Road came into existence – through high places barely fit for habitation: windy, bleak and far from water. Pig Cottage was reputed to be haunted – passers-by would report strange blue flickering flames burning within – but that was when it was derelict, and had no doors and windows, and the local farmer used it to sty his pigs. The methane from their slurry would on occasion spontaneously ignite. The council had eventually requisitioned the place, allegedly to house the troublesome Nutwich family, though some said to annoy the water company. There was no electricity, no piped gas – but the Water Board, under new regulations imposed upon it by the Government, had been obliged to provide a water supply, at great cost. Mrs Nutwich had eight children, of whom Theresa was the youngest but by no means the biggest. By some trick of the genes – her side, for the children were by different fathers – all were well above six foot tall, and broad, strong and pale with it: slow and amiable. Ned said it was nothing to do with genes: it was the pig slurry did it.

Alexandra could see the problem of remaining in the neighbourhood. Everywhere she went she would remember something Ned had said, or done, and be humiliated because what she had thought special to her was not. Where she had seen him-and-her, Ned had seen him-and-her-her-her. She, Alexandra, was diminished by an equivalent fraction of the number of 'hers'. If there were too many she might all but vanish away, dwindled to the point of invisibility.

Alexandra had dropped off and collected Theresa often enough. She had never been inside the house. The Nutwiches were known to be private people. But now the door was opened by a very pregnant young woman, fine-boned enough to snap, skinny and small except for the vast bump in her middle, tight under stretched fabric. She would be one of the boys' wives; a privileged stranger. Alexandra hoped the birth wouldn't prove difficult.

The room was small, square, cosy and stuffy; a three-piece suite in an orange checked fabric; comfy chairs drawn up round the TV; a round table, a Madonna in a gold frame, bleeding hearts on the walls. Over the table was her, Alexandra's, best lace table-cloth (Belgium, 1835, approx. £230). A fire burned in the grate, glittering on Ned's copper fire-tongs in their stand (1910 Arts and Crafts, £550). A Victorian birdcage with a canary in it, singing. So this was where the birdcage (1851, Great Exhibition style, £900) had gone. It had disappeared, mysteriously, from the barn, though no one had been quite sure when.

Theresa came down the stairs slowly; thud-thud-thud. She scowled at her pregnant sister-in-law.

'We don't let people in here,' Theresa said. 'This is our place.'
'Sorry,' said the pregnant girl, and scuttled.
'I know what you're thinking,' said Theresa. 'It's not the way it looks.'
'I'm not thinking anything,' said Alexandra, wishing she had not come round, not come in. 'Though I would like the table-cloth back, some time. No hurry.'
'You just shove it in the wash,' said Theresa. 'I look after it properly. It's so delicate. It's antique. It's safer here.'

'All the same,' said Alexandra, mildly.

'So, what do you want?' asked Theresa. On her home ground she seemed a different person. More bad-tempered, more aggressive. 'All the way up here! It's my day off. I deserve some peace. I've been upset too. You think you're the only one, but you're not.'

Alexandra said she understood that: everyone was in quite a state. She explained to Theresa that Sascha wouldn't be back for a week: could Theresa hold on for that long? Theresa said she supposed so, if Mrs Ludd didn't mind paying her to waste her time.

Alexandra said she didn't. She would need help sorting Ned's clothes. Perhaps Theresa could come down to The Cottage and help her, and then she wouldn't be wasting her time.

Theresa said she wasn't paid to sort through dead people's clothes, she was paid for child care.

Theresa sat down in an armchair, pushing the arms out with her bulk as she did so. They were already half-off: effectively, they were hinged. Alexandra sat in the chair opposite. A small child with a grubby face and bare legs ran between them, and pinched some potato crisps from a glass bowl which Alexandra observed to be her own, leaded crystal, French, *circa* 1705, £830. Theresa slapped the child's legs as she ran off. The hand was large: the blow sudden. The child let out a howl.

'Don't worry, I don't hit yours,' Theresa said. 'Ned said not to so I don't, but life with Sascha would be a lot easier if someone did. That kid is spoiled rotten.'

'I don't understand what you mean by *spoiling*,' said Alexandra. 'Do explain.'

'You are a sarcastic bitch,' shouted Theresa, getting to her feet. The chair came with her. Theresa had to knock it away from her flesh. One of the arms finally detached itself so it fell separately. 'Mr Ludd gave me all these things. You can't prove he didn't.'

'I'm not giving them a second thought,' said Alexandra.

'Who do you think you are, anyway?' said Theresa. 'You never loved Ned, you don't even love your own child. Everyone knew that. You just had him to save your marriage. Why bother to have a baby at all if you just give it to someone else to look after? That's what beats me.'

'Because I have to work,' said Alexandra. She could see that without Ned's presence in the house Theresa as child care was impossible. She had already given in: she could hardly be bothered to fight.

'You don't have to work,' said Theresa. 'No one has to work. You just love it, your face in the papers. If you wanted to, you could live off benefits like everyone else, but you don't want to. You have to be someone special. You have to have someone like me to be better than, so you can boss them about. I'm so sorry for that poor little boy: he needs a firm hand and a visit to a psychologist. He's disturbed.'

'It was your red bracelet on the bed,' said Alexandra. 'Just your style. If it isn't stolen, it's plastic.'

'Nothing happened,' said Theresa. 'I swear it on my life.'

Alexandra wanted to ask the nature of the non-happening but in the end didn't. What was the point of that either?

'I guess we've reached the parting of the ways,' she said.

29

Alexandra called by the morgue. Ned had company now. A metal trolley on wheels had been placed next to his. A small group of shocked relatives stood and stared at the body of a thin, elderly woman. Her jaw was bound to keep it closed. It was strange, thought Alexandra, how few people seemed to die, considering everyone did; how few dead bodies a living person encountered; how shocking it was when they did.

Alexandra had never hit Ned in life: though he had hit her once, during the herpes episode. But she hadn't taken it badly; rather she had taken responsibility for his state of mind. She had assumed he was part of her, she an extension of him. She thought perhaps women minding men hitting them was a recent cultural innovation: in the past women had never tried to be separate from their husbands, or claim their separate personality. The aim was to incorporate, not stay distinguished. His flesh yours, your flesh his. But Ned's death had put a stop to all that. So far as she was concerned, his part of the union was dead, hers went on living. Separation, individuality, had been forced upon her. She would have hit him now but could hardly do so in front of the old lady's relatives. One was meant to respect the dead, unless the Government declared them an official enemy, in which case you just shovelled them into common graves so you didn't get the plague. Alexandra aimed a quick kick at the trolley wheels instead: the trolley clanged into the end wall. Ned's body shuddered, but stayed in place. She walked out. The others stared after her, further bewildered.

30

Alexandra called at Elder House. Abbie's coolness had evaporated. She greeted her friend with a hug. Arthur wasn't there. He had taken the students on a coach trip to Lyme Regis, where they were to have cream teas and look at Jane Austen's house. Abbie was making plum jam. The air in the kitchen was full of a pungent sweetness. Abbie hoped the plums were not too ripe. They should have been picked a week earlier.

'But you were looking after me,' said Alexandra. 'So they stayed on the bough.'

'True,' said Abbie. 'But being with you at such a time was the most important thing of all. We're friends.'

'But you were angry with me yesterday,' said Alexandra, 'and now you're not. Why's that?'

Abbie didn't reply. So Alexandra described to her, complete with mime and appropriate facial expressions, the circumstances in which she had fired Theresa.

'I always knew Theresa was hopeless,' said Abbie. 'You're so easily conned, Alexandra, you can hardly blame others when they do it.' And Abbie went on at some length as to how Theresa had been OK while Ned was there to keep an eye on things, but now what was she, Alexandra, to do: she couldn't just land Sascha with a stranger at a time like this; he'd be traumatised enough; losing his father, his mother away all week. Babies were one thing: you could pay through the nose and get qualified nannies, but four-year-olds knew too much of what was going on ever to be shuffled off and not know it. Alexandra would just have to give up work for a time. Abbie knew Alexandra would be bored stiff in the country. She'd miss the thrills and the publicity and the media attention, but once a woman had a child, she was a mother first and foremost, and Alexandra must put Sascha before anything. Otherwise she was being selfish.

'The great modern sin,' said Alexandra. 'Being selfish.'

Abbie said that Alexandra must allow herself time to grieve, settle down in The Cottage and make it a happy home for Sascha. And be sure not to fall into anyone else's arms too soon. But Alexandra would have all her friends around her to protect her. People who loved her.

'Oh yes,' said Alexandra. 'Them. The jam's burning.'

A smell of scorching filled the air, mixed with sweetness. Alexandra quite liked it. But Abbie squealed and rushed to attend to it. She heaved the great steel pan off the stove to the side of the sink, and as swiftly as she could transferred the still-bubbling, viscous contents to a succession of smaller pans: pouring when she could, ladling when she couldn't. It was dangerous work.

'Don't burn yourself,' said Alexandra. Abbie looked at her friend uneasily, and while she lost concentration slopped a splodge of still-scalding jam on to her sandalled toe and the bare and tender skin of her upper foot. How she hopped about!

'You and Arthur and Ned and Jenny were planning a property deal, I hear,' said Alexandra.

'Who did you hear that from?' asked Abbie, startled. She had ice in a plastic bag and was applying it to her foot.

'Mr Quatrop,' said Alexandra.

'Oh,' said Abbie.

'What was I meant to do?' asked Alexandra. 'Or didn't you think of that?'

'We thought of it a lot,' said Abbie. 'Believe me, we worried about you all the time. But you would have had the London flat. You were always so happy there, Ned said. It was all just speculation. Testing the water. If you and Ned were to get divorced –'

'Takes two to divorce,' said Alexandra.

'But Ned said you and he were talking about it.'

'Always the humorist,' said Alexandra.

'Believe me, Alexandra,' said Abbie. 'I only wanted your happiness. Ned just didn't deserve you. It was horrible, what was going on behind your back. You've no idea.'

'Wouldn't it have been simpler just to tell me?' asked Alexandra.

Abbie abandoned the jam altogether and started crying, bending over her blistering toe. The sandal strap had stuck to it.

'I didn't have the courage. Nobody did. Somebody had to do something to bring things to a head, so I thought this was it. You might just about notice a For Sale sign going up. I don't know why one does things. Ned could be so persuasive.'

'But I would never have given my permission,' said Alexandra. 'Ned knew that. He knew how I loved The Cottage. It's my home. What would I want to be involved with a Theatrical Design Centre for, Abbie?'

'Perhaps he thought you wouldn't want to be,' said Abbie. 'Perhaps he thought you'd just drift off to London and the Sloane Square house. Perhaps he thought he didn't need your permission to sell.'

She kept her eyes lowered. Her foot was flaring nastily. The ice cubes hurt too much to keep in place. Alexandra thought a little before she spoke.

'It's possible the house is in Ned's name only,' said Alexandra. 'I realise that. But he and I were married and have a child. Any court will recognise my claim to live in it.'

'That's OK then,' said Abbie, flatly. 'Jenny's like a steamroller when she gets her tiny teeth into something.'

'She got her teeth into Eric Stenstrom's dick a year or two back,' said Alexandra, 'and turned it inside out. Did you know about that?'

Abbie said she didn't, with an expression both so helpless and aghast that Alexandra believed her.

'I saw your name up on Dr Moebius's screen,' said Alexandra. 'I guess you went into the surgery in a real hurry when you heard my name linked with Eric Stenstrom.'

'His partner died of AIDS,' said Abbie. 'Dr Moebius said I was right to worry. I wasn't being neurotic. He said he'd hurry the results through for me. I was in such a state!'

'Why? Because you'd fucked with a man who'd been fucked by a woman who'd been fucked by a man who might have had AIDS?'

'Yes,' said Abbie. 'I'm so ashamed.'

'I think you should get the plum tree cut down,' said Alexandra. 'It brings no one any luck.'

Abbie pulled herself together, hobbled to the sink, and started cleaning the bottom of the big steel pan of its blackened layer of caramelised cooked plums. Wasps began to congregate. Alexandra had one on her hand. Let it crawl.

'You were with Ned when he died,' said Alexandra. 'It wasn't Jenny at all. She came into the bedroom and found you fucking my husband, and that's when he had his heart attack.'

Abbie had the bottom of the pan smooth. She dried it out carefully. Then she began to empty pan after pan of semi-liquid plum jam back into it.

'Jenny's excessive hysterics,' said Alexandra, 'your excessive house-cleaning. These things come to one.'

'It was only the once,' said Abbie. 'Honestly. Only the once.'

Alexandra sighed.

'I did it for you, Alexandra,' said Abbie. 'To break the Jenny spell.'

Alexandra laughed.

'You couldn't have borne it, Alexandra. I saved you from it. Having Ned die all over me. I'm glad for you it happened that way. I am your friend. I'd do anything for you.'

'Thank you, Abbie.'

'Don't be sarcastic, Alexandra, on top of everything. You don't know how important you are to me. Please!'

'And you hung around to mock me and keep secrets, and conspire, having learned the habit from Ned, I suppose?'

'I hung around to look after you, Alexandra; I knew you'd be devastated. Better you thought it was Jenny than me, your best friend. Best of all no one. But that didn't work.'

'You probably didn't want to face Arthur too soon. You might have told him the truth.'

'I do tend to blurt it out,' said Abbie.

'Yes, you do,' said Alexandra. 'I wish you didn't. It was only another far-fetched theory of mine, waiting for denial. Now look. Does Vilna know?'

Abbie shook her head. She put the big pan and its contents on the stove and started swilling out the lesser containers. Boiling jam had splashed everywhere in Abbie's haste to save at least some of the batch from contamination, from the taste of burning, and the sticky stuff had now congealed. Alexandra finally rose from her chair to help Abbie. She took a sharp, short kitchen knife and started easing off the deep purple drips from tiles and cooker.

'And now the whole world believes Ned died in Jenny Linden's arms,' said Alexandra, 'because she tells them so. She wants to own him in death as she never could in life. And she's got her husband back and she's laughing.'

'Yes,' said Abbie.

'You played into her hands, Abbie,' said Alexandra, 'by not telling the truth.'

'I'm sorry,' said Abbie.

'And no one's told Arthur,' said Alexandra.

'Of course not,' said Abbie, shocked.

'Well, well,' said Alexandra.

'It was you Ned loved,' said Abbie. 'He talked about you all the time. It's just you were away so often and Jenny was there in front of him all the time, lying down with her legs open.'

'I think she was very important to him,' said Alexandra. 'At least at one time.' Worst fears!

'But I wasn't important,' said Abbie, hopefully.

'You were still in my bed,' said Alexandra. The knife didn't seem so short any more, and it squeaked against the ceramic as if it were very sharp. She raised it.

'I was set up,' said Abbie, 'by Ned. I think he wanted to put Jenny off. He wanted her to discover us together.'

'And he died in the set-up,' said Alexandra. 'He came and then he went.'

'He came and then he went,' repeated Abbie, and gave her friend a small, shy smile, which to her astonishment was returned. Alexandra lowered the knife and went back to the jam splashes.

31

Abbie hobbled out to see Alexandra off. Now Abbie's foot had been dressed and bandaged by her friend, she felt comforted, as scoured out of blame as her steel preserving pan had been scoured of caramelised jam. She hurt but she was OK.

'If there's anything I can do,' Abbie said. The last of the plums had been dropping on to the roof of Alexandra's car.
'I'm serious about the plum tree,' said Alexandra. 'It ought to go. It brings bad luck.'
'But the blossom is so pretty,' said Abbie, 'and the Japanese students like to draw it.'
'Even so,' said Alexandra. 'Get rid of it.'
Abbie nodded.
'There is something else you can do for me,' said Alexandra, and explained.
Abbie wailed.
'But I can't, Alexandra. I would if I could, but I don't have the time. How can I cope with a small child as well as everything else?'
'By buying jam from the shop instead of making it yourself; that kind of thing,' said Alexandra. 'By giving up your domestic affectations, because that's all they are. This is a world of convenience foods and microwaves.'
Abbie whimpered.
'Sascha will be at full-time nursery school,' Alexandra comforted her. 'You'll have Sundays and Mondays off while I'm home. Only five days a week till the end of the *Doll's House* run. Then I'm home full-time. Until the next part comes along.'
'But Sascha's a handful, everyone knows!'

'He'll remind you of Ned,' said Alexandra.

'Oh don't, don't!' There were tears in Abbie's eyes. 'Please!'

'But I won't tell Arthur that,' said Alexandra. She had lost ten pounds in the last week. Her eyes were larger than usual.

'It's blackmail,' said Abbie.

'I prefer to call it expiation,' said Alexandra.

'OK, OK, OK,' said Abbie. 'All right, I will.'

On the way home in the car Alexandra felt the familiar state of suspension descending; the landscape passed to either side as in a dream, not quite real. She was being propelled over water with a swift, smooth, silent motion, as clouds in a speeded-up film, towards the silent shore where Ned had disappeared: she was still in the light but the edge of the fog was near. Too near. She pulled into the nearest lay-by. She wanted to stay alive. Well, she supposed that was an advance. She slept a little. Woke. Worst fears, Leah had said. Expiation, she herself had said. Cows were being driven down the road: they were passing the car. It was in their way. They barged into its sides with their gaunt brown hairy flanks; concave where they ought to be convex; their monstrous udders swung from side to side, banged against their legs. Hormone supplements made the udders gigantic, stretched to bursting: they were on their way to be milked. Machines would do it – would offer relief – pull and relax, pull and relax. Heavy breath from black rubber nostrils patched the car windows with moist droplets. Huge red-veined brown eyes stared at her, not unkindly, but with a dreadful resigned and female melancholy. Our troubles are worse than yours.

These days farmers would just run the bull with the herd, not keep him trampling, macho and furious, tethered in the yard. In a field with sixty cows the bull is placid, properly serviced, properly servicing. Sex for all keeps everyone quiet. Perhaps that had been Ned's notion.

The attacks of non-affect, of suspension, came less frequently and lasted for a shorter time than they had a week ago. Nor was the blocking-out of experience so intense. A boy with a dog followed up behind the herd: his task to drive the cows to the milking sheds, lucky old them. Woollen cap, muddy boots, old shirt, ancient trousers: long greasy hair, a sweet face. She even recognised him: Kevin Crump. She'd done some work five years back with the school drama class. Kevin had been its bright star. A good singing voice; a good stage presence, though always trouble with his lines. Now this. At least he had a job. She wound down the window.

'You OK, Mrs Ludd?' He was concerned for her.

'Sleepy, that's all,' she said. 'I took a bit of shut-eye. Dangerous to keep driving.'

He nodded. He found an old piece of paper in a pocket, a biro. He handed them to her through the window.

'Could I have your autograph?' he asked, tentatively. 'Now you're famous?'

'Sure.' She signed her name: the biro was on the brink of running out. 'Ludd' didn't seem to belong to her any more; it was appropriate that the word came faintly and she had to write over the two 'd's' to make them legible. A mess. But so were his cows; not that it was his fault. So was she a mess, and it probably was her fault.

'Thanks.' He was hugely pleased, and passed on.

Worst fears. The curse of Leah.

Jenny Linden's importance: Abbie's unimportance. Alexandra had acknowledged that herself, without thinking. That it wasn't sex, it was love. That Ned loved Jenny Linden. That at the sudden sound of Jenny Linden's voice Ned's soul would lurch. That when she came through a door his heart would lift. She could make him happy just by existing. That Ned would lie to and deceive Alexandra not because it turned him on sexually – that had been Jenny Linden's interpretation, as she squirmed and wriggled and tried to hurt, and Alexandra had accepted it too easily, as the least hurtful of all options – but simply because Ned wanted to see Jenny, longed to see Jenny, had to see her, hear her, touch her, be with her. Because he hurt so when he was apart from her. That the hurt left when he was with her.

That he had taken Alexandra to Jenny Linden's house only because he couldn't get rid of Alexandra and he had to see Jenny Linden, be with Jenny Linden, so the hurt would stop. And because in the light of this love she, Alexandra, counted as nothing. That Ned had loved Jenny Linden.

Worst fears.

That in the belief that a woman had to be beautiful, and sensuous, and witty, and wonderful, in order to trigger real love, erotic love, the kind of emotional drama that ran through to the heart of the universe, the hot line to the source of life itself, the in-love kind, Alexandra had been wrong. More, she had shown herself to be vain, and foolish, and shallow, and Ned had noticed. Not that his noticing had anything to do with it. You did not love necessarily where you admired: or cease to love when admiration failed. Love came and it went; it was there or it wasn't. The blessing of the gods, and their curse.

Worst fears.

Jenny had not pursued, Ned had pursued. Ned had broken Dave and Jenny's marriage; Dave was right. Jenny was a child, easily influenced; Ned's victim. Ned in love. Now Ned was gone, Jenny was back with Dave.

Worst fears.

Best hopes? There were none. Start by saying Ned had fallen out of love with Jenny Linden: end by saying, but that instead of turning back to Alexandra, Ned had invited Abbie into his bed.

Alexandra started the car and drove back to The Cottage. On the way Mr Lightfoot's private ambulance passed, travelling swiftly in the other direction. No doubt it had Ned's body in it, with any luck neatly contained in a coffin (oak, current, £480), on the way to town for tomorrow's funeral and cremation. The coffin would pick up a proper hearse at the other end: black, grand and glossy, but underpowered. A twenty-mile journey by hearse when you were dead made you a source of traffic hold-ups, especially up hills, and was discouraged by the police.

32

The day of the funeral dawned bright and clear. Abbie drove
Vilna down. They had patched up their quarrel, at Alexandra's
insistence. Vilna wore a smart black suit with self-coloured braid-
ing and a deep, scooped neckline. She wore a crimson gauze
scarf to veil her bosom.

'It isn't modesty, darling,' she said. 'My tits are getting scraggy,
like my neck. They must only show in candlelight. I have had
to do without my special beauty treatment for so long. It is
tragic.'

'What is your special beauty treatment?' asked Abbie. Arthur
was travelling down separately in the school's mini-bus, dropping
two students off at the station on the way. Fond as he was of
Vilna, Arthur said, he would find her a difficult companion on
the way to a funeral. Her self-preoccupation would be troublesome, when they were meant to be thinking about Ned. So if
Abbie didn't mind? Abbie didn't mind. 'Sperm,' said Vilna.
'Sperm is the best beauty treatment of all. Essence of male. I
have been deprived of it for so long. I am falling to pieces.
Wrinkles are appearing. What can I do? My mother spies on
me. Clive pays her to, I know he does. It is a very bitter thing;
one's own mother to keep one prisoner.'

It was true, Abbie thought, that lately Vilna had seemed to age.
Haggard was beginning to turn into gaunt; smooth olive skin to
papery grey. And Maria always pottered about in the background, scarcely letting Vilna out of her sight.

'Only another six months, Vilna,' she said, 'and Clive will be
home.'

'Supposing he's forgotten how to do it?' demanded Vilna. 'Or has become a homosexual? That happens to men in prison. What then?'

'I expect you could sue,' said Abbie, 'for loss of looks.'

Abbie concentrated on her driving. She was wearing Vilna's navy blue with the hem tacked up. It would do. She could see herself in the driving mirror: shiny, wavy hair; bright eyes; agreeably healthy freckles. She was pleased with what she saw.

'You're looking good,' said Vilna. 'Hadn't you noticed? Extra-special essence of dying man. Very rare.'

Abbie's hands tightened on the wheel. She always drove care-fully, both hands where they should be – ten o'clock and two o'clock, and no hand-over-hand on a sharp turn.

'Only a joke,' said Vilna. 'You English have no sense of humour. What can one do but laugh?'

Abbie didn't reply and they drove to the funeral in silence, broken only by Vilna's directions as she followed the map drawn and distributed by Hamish; it was not noticeably to scale, in spite of Hamish's reputation for precision.

'Jenny told me everything,' said Vilna, as they turned into the crematorium gates. 'Now she is back with her husband, she is glad that Ned died on you and not on her.'

'Jenny is a hopeless witness,' said Abbie eventually, 'about every-thing.' It was going to be a popular funeral. Most of the parking spaces were already gone, and they were half an hour early.

'She is,' said Vilna, 'and of course I shall say so to anyone who asks. I shall say that Jenny is too full of emotion to tell fact from fiction. That's what I will say. Friendship is important, no? Even in this hopeless land? And we are friends, you and I, are we not?'

Abbie could see that this was going to have to be the case from now on. There could be no cutting Vilna; Vilna would have to be asked to the Hunt Ball – for which she, Abbie, more or less controlled the invitation list. Where she, Abbie, went – to a private view at a morgue, to a Private View at an art show, to a charity performance in the local stately home, to lunch at the Priory with the monks – Vilna would have to come along. She would be accepted into society, however local, however boring. That was to be Vilna's price for secrecy, for helping to deny all to Arthur, just as looking after Sascha was the price Alexandra would charge. Abbie laid her hand on Vilna's knee. It was not too high or unendurable a price.

'We're friends,' she said. 'Of course we are.'

Crowds gathered outside the chapel. Friends, relatives, hangers-on, the invited and the uninvited. The press were there: sudden flashes from unseen cameras; tiny tape recorders in hiding hands. Unobtrusive. 'We do not wish to intrude into private grief – but –' Theatre people, publishers, agents; the Preservation of Ancient Rights, Ancient Roads, Ancient Graveyards Committee people, quango people – Ned's work on the Performing Arts panel: Ibsen people, Norwegian people. A man in his time can play many parts. People whom Ned had savaged in reviews; crocodile-tear people. Music people; ancient-instrument people. Inland Revenue people, incognito. Antique dealers, junk dealers. Actors of both sexes. All sexes. People from the Central Hospital for Venereal Diseases (Ned had organised a charity show). The chapel filled. There was no room inside for more. The doors were closed once the coffin was in. Loudspeakers were quickly rigged for those outside. The service was broadcast to the air, to the trees, to the circling birds, to other mourners altogether. *For All the Saints, Lord of the Dance.* An extract from *The Master Builder.* Hamish had decided well. Short speeches from friends.

Then 'Sailing By' as the coffin slipped in between the parted curtains, into the flaming furnace which by implication waited, but in fact did not. The actual burning of corpses was done in two sessions a week; but of course one body at a time, to keep the ashes separate. So it was claimed. No one, by tradition, believed it. Otherwise the weight of the ashes was too heavy a burden for the bereaved to bear.

'Sailing By' – a liquid, silly tune, played every half past midnight as the national radio station closed down, and had been since

167

the beginning of radio time. An apology for silence, a sweetly soporific melody to rock you to sleep, to drive out thoughts of revolution, to drown protest with nostalgia. As common as the cinema organ is common: second-rate as a plagiarism must be second-rate, a sound to induce a groan in a musician and a sigh in the sentimental. Alexandra's choice. Hamish had begged her: at least some intervention, some contribution, please! You were his wife: don't leave all this to me, his brother. There was some consternation among the guests, a giggle or two, nervous: but the tune had its merits, the association soothed. Cremations were always like this. They lacked the solemnity of a graveside burial. There was always something tacky, mass-market, about them. But it was a good funeral, everyone agreed. And a memorial service still to come.

Alexandra? Where was Alexandra? The press wanted to know. 'Over there,' her friends said, pointing. 'Over there.' But she wasn't.

Jenny Linden was there, dressed in scarlet (as Leah advised), weeping and wailing, copiously, next to the aisle in the front pew.

Leah was there, dressed in pure white; a thinner version of Jenny.

Dave Linden was present; his wife had insisted. But he stayed outside the chapel. Abbie was there, and Vilna, and Arthur. Dr Moebius was there, and of course Hamish. Daisy Longriff was there, crying softly and leaning on colleagues from the theatre. Dressed in black from tip to toe; stretch fabric over her beautiful bosom, vinyl elsewhere. The press took many photographs. Daisy posed all over the place; before, after and even during the ceremony.

The postman was there. He was wearing Ned's shoes, beautifully polished. So was Mr Quatrop there, and Mr and Mrs Paddle from the stationer's shop. Chrissie was there, and Hamish embraced her.

Those who knew this or that glanced at one another, raised an eyebrow, or looked carefully away, and were pleased enough that Alexandra wasn't there: the whole event was embarrassing enough without the burden of her presence.

Irene wasn't there.
Theresa wasn't there.
All kinds of others weren't there. The world went on. Alexandra, concerned with its continued turning, was in London seeing the casting director about the possibility of playing opposite Michael Douglas in his new film. He offered her the part, but she felt she had to decline. She couldn't take her child to Hollywood, not at such a juncture in his life. Her home and her life were here in England. But it was nice to be asked.

On the evening of the day Alexandra missed Ned's funeral, she went to see Daisy Longriff in *A Doll's House*. The theatre was not dark, after all. She needed diversion. And she wanted her part back.

She supposed that Ned still maintained a corporeal presence on this earth. His body now lay on some other slab or trolley, still waiting for the furnace. The open season for viewing was over; that was all that had changed. No one would bother to keep the beret on over his split skull. Should his eyes fly open, no one would cover them. Appearances need no longer be preserved. With every day that passed he would, she felt, mind less. Nor would she know when the body was consumed by fire and turned to ashes. It scarcely mattered. Ned had left it long ago, in any case, was still trudging up the mountainside, through the grim forest. She suspected that without her blessing he would trudge for ever. Serve him right for not looking back.

Alexandra arrived at the theatre at seven o'clock. Performances started at eight, instead of seven-forty-five. Alexandra had missed only eight performances. In her absence management had been busy. There was someone new at the box office – a bad-tempered, middle-aged woman with a fleshy face and permed hair – who made her pay for her ticket, saying, 'Alexandra who?' and flicking through envelopes in order to be able to say in triumph, 'Nothing here,' deaf to Alexandra's protests that there wouldn't be anyway. It was true that Alexandra had arrived at the theatre without warning, but she took the unpleasantness as a bad omen. She had planned another four weeks' absence, which would give herself and Sascha time to settle to a life without Ned. But if you could be so forgotten in eight days, forcibly retired to the country as a 'serious' actor – in other words worthy, dull and about to be given an OBE – what could not happen in four weeks?

There were already new red stickers plastered over the original tasteful stickers, which had been, all agreed, unspeakably dreary in classic greys, blacks and duns. 'Daisy Longriff now as Nora', and fresh quotes from critics, 'Daisy Longriff's Tarantella – the sexiest lead in town' now hid 'Alexandra Ludd's Nora – a searing performance' and 'a Nora to remember, moving and powerful'.

Alexandra went back to the box office and asked what the advance bookings were like, but the woman with the permed hair did not seem to hear. I don't exist, thought Alexandra. Ned has taken me with him. Propelled on his penis, flying through the air, both of us dissolved into nothingness. It was strange that his prick seemed the only substantial thing of either of them which remained: that piece of flesh and muscle, that original source of warmth, still had enough power to transport her. Another pun, she thought, and fainted.

Sam the front-of-house manager helped her up and took her to his office. He had straight yellow hair and round glasses: he was a dead ringer for David Hockney.

'Oh,' said the woman from the box office. 'Alexandra *Ludd*. Why didn't you *say*?'

Sam seemed put out that Alexandra had not been to Ned's funeral. He was sure she would regret it.

'Never,' said Alexandra, 'I am too proud. I never knew I was so proud.' She'd thought of herself as a humble little thing, dismissing her celebrity as meaningless, a by-product of the world's folly. But that turned out to be Ned's view: a cloak worn as a disguise, chosen by him, not both of them together. When it came to it, she was not one to go to a husband's funeral and put up with the clamorous weeping of a host of other women who turned up to claim him too. Especially if they were as plain as Jenny Linden, or as vulgar as Daisy Longriff, or as countrified as Abbie Carpenter. The audience – for so she saw the mourners – would wink and nudge and stare and wonder what Ned saw in them when he had Alexandra waiting at home and she would be the more humiliated and demeaned, and they, resentful of her success, would rejoice at her comeuppance.

'Who would you want him to have as a mistress?' Sam asked. 'Princess Di?'

'Not even for Princess Di,' said Alexandra, 'would I have gone to Ned's funeral.'

Sam remarked that she, Alexandra, was a hard bitch. He seemed to admire her. Alexandra said she wished she had had Ned buried, not cremated. Then she could have slipped into some graveyard by night, and sat there and come to terms with the corruption of the flesh; and the slithering in and out of worms. It was more difficult to sit and contemplate an urn of ashes. Sam said they mostly came not in urns but in navy-blue boxes tied with gold band: his mother had been returned to him like this. When were they going to actually burn the body? Did Alexandra know?

Alexandra said she thought they already had: just some minutes ago, when she had fainted. Sam said that was pure fantasy. Alexandra agreed. She had become better at agreeing over the last week. It preserved energy. She asked Sam whether the advance bookings were good or bad.

'Good,' he said.

'Daisy Longriff gives a good performance?' asked Alexandra, only just able to stop herself adding, 'better than mine?'

Sam said that Daisy Longriff's performance was crap, but the advance bookings were good, very good. He suggested that

Alexandra didn't speak to management direct but let Harry Barney do it. Technically, Alexandra had no right to take time off for a bereavement: she was in breach of contract. Nor had she produced a medical certificate within the three days allowed, which would have been her most sensible course of action in the circumstances.

'But they'd never stick by the letter of the contract,' said Alexandra. 'It would be inhuman.'

Sam pointed out that theatrical management was inhuman by definition. 'The show must go on' was a management *diktat* which kept actors on the stage through air-raids and terminal illness, and management in profit. Frankly, he doubted Alexandra would have Nora's part back.

'Why did no one warn me?' asked Alexandra. 'Remind me about the medical certificate; at the very least?'

Sam hummed and hawed and finally said he supposed it was because everyone wanted a long run, and transfer to a bigger theatre, and with Daisy Longriff as Nora it might just happen. Times were hard.

Alexandra agreed that they were.

Daisy Longriff drifted in. She was wearing Alexandra's great-grandmother's wedding dress, which Alexandra had lent the theatre. It was white silk and had a low neckline and a full skirt. This was the dress, worn in the Tarantella scene, out of which Alexandra's bosom had fallen on the first night. She wondered why Daisy was wearing it, since it was by now seven-forty and in the opening scene Nora comes in from a shopping trip in a small Norwegian town. She did not ask Daisy. She did not want to know the answer.

Daisy said she'd heard Alexandra had fainted in the lobby. She hoped she was all right. She, Daisy, sympathised: she had been all the way to poor Ned's funeral and back that day, and she was completely wrung out. But the show must go on. Alexandra said she supposed it must.

Daisy said wasn't it strange, when Ned had been alive she'd felt really guilty about Alexandra but now he was dead all that had stopped. She just felt glad she'd been able to offer Ned all that wonderful intensity of sexual experience. Life was so short! Alexandra said she was glad Daisy was glad. Sam tried to hustle Daisy away, saying he'd heard the call for beginners. Daisy told Sam to stop trying to be tactful, it was embarrassing, she and Alexandra understood each other.

'If you wear that dress for the opening scene,' said Alexandra, 'what do you wear for the Tarantella?'

'A mini-skirt and black boots,' said Daisy, 'and that's all. She's trying to win back Torvald from Dr Rank.'

'Oh I see,' said Alexandra, 'and I suppose Nora's a lesbian at heart?'

'Of course,' said Daisy. 'That way the whole play makes sense. It's a revelation! Poor Ned will turn in his grave, but he's dead. I have to be careful, or I start crying.'

'Ned doesn't have a grave,' said Alexandra, 'he's just ashes.'

'You are too literal, Alexandra,' protested Daisy. 'Ned always told me how literal you were.'

And she bounced away to go on stage, her bosom already out of Alexandra's great-grandmother's wedding dress.

'We'd better find you your seat,' said Sam.

'I don't think I'll bother,' said Alexandra.

She spent the night at Angliss Street. There was no sign of Chrissie, but Chrissie's clothes were in the wardrobe and Alexandra's had been placed on the spare bed. The furniture had been rearranged, slightly. It was apparent to Alexandra that Chrissie did not mean to go away.

She dreamed of Ned. She was at The Cottage, standing on the path outside the kitchen window. She looked in and saw Jenny Linden making tea and Ned at the table, with Sascha on his knee. She shouted and shouted at the window but nobody could hear, and nobody saw her. She screamed really loudly with a terrible effort – she was the woman in the stolen Munch painting – and woke up to hear herself making only a little squeaky noise.

She drove back early to The Cottage. She stopped in Eddon

173

Gurney to buy milk and a local newspaper. Inside was a feature on Ned's funeral, a double-page spread, with a large photograph of Jenny Linden weeping, and underneath the caption 'Alexandra Ludd mourns'. Someone must have pointed out the mistake in time, so it had not made the national press.

Coming across the page by accident, Alexandra laughed.

33

Alexandra laughed so hard, in fact, she fell off her chair. It was small, hard and shiny. The day was really hot, and she wore a skimpy cotton dress and no stockings, so the hard plastic stuck to the back of her thighs. She was glad enough to fall off.

'You're hysterical,' said Hamish, crossly, but she showed him the photograph and he all but laughed himself. They were sitting waiting in Sheldon Smythe's offices.

'If you'd been at the funeral,' he said crossly, 'it wouldn't have happened. You're going to be sorry in due course. It was a terrible thing to do. No one doesn't go to their husband's funeral, no matter what happened in the past.'

'I'm sorry, Hamish,' said Alexandra. She could see the virtue of contrition. 'But so many people! And the press were there in force. I took one look and slipped away. I just couldn't face it.'

He forgave her.

'You've had a hard time,' he acknowledged.

Sheldon Smythe's offices were up from the supermarket, down from Mrs Paddle in the stationer's, next to Mr Lightfoot's. Now Ned's body was no longer in the morgue, the curve of the road seemed less numinous; quite everyday and ordinary; business-like. Sheldon Smythe was new to the area. He came out of his offices, and though a stranger to Alexandra, offered her his condolences. He had read the obituaries, he said. He was a small, dapper man with a round face and heavy eyelids. 'A great loss,' he said. He had read an account of the funeral in the local paper. A great and special event, apparently. He seemed already to have met Hamish, which surprised Alexandra, but she did not care to show it.

When Hamish and Alexandra followed Sheldon Smythe into his inner office, she found Jenny and Dave Linden sitting with their backs to the wall, holding hands. Again, she declined to show her surprise.

'Something funny?' asked Jenny. 'We could hear you.'

'Fairly funny,' said Alexandra. The hot weather was breaking. Through Sheldon Smythe's window she could see really black and powerful clouds gathering. Filing cabinets lined up against plastered walls which sheer age had rendered barely straight. Spiders were plentiful. The computer on the desk seemed incongruous, out of place. Once this had been someone's living room, lit by candle or, later, oil-lamp, at first heated by nothing at all in the days when people kept close to one another for warmth – later by a fire in a grate. Alexandra wondered what dramas had been enacted here in the past; she feared to consider what might happen today.

'Why is Jenny Linden here?' asked Alexandra, to the company in general.

'Mrs Linden is here because Mr Ludd's will affects her,' said Sheldon Smythe. He tended to close his eyes when he spoke. They drooped as if thought wearied him. He rocked to and fro in his chair, a habit Irene had always warned Alexandra against. Presently he would snap one of the back legs but what business was that of Alexandra's?

'We find ourselves in a strange situation here,' said Sheldon Smythe. And he explained to Alexandra that her husband had bequeathed The Cottage to Jenny Linden.

'He can't do that,' said Alexandra sharply. 'It's the matrimonial home.'

Sheldon Smythe remarked that the property had never been put in Alexandra's name, presumably by intention. There was no reason to believe Mr Ludd had ever been anything other than in his right mind.

'Even so,' said Alexandra, 'I'm his wife and have his child and the courts will protect me. The world isn't daft.' But she didn't like the smug expression on Jenny Linden's face, and the wretched one on that of Jenny Linden's husband, as if he knew only too well what was going to happen next. Hamish peered enigmatically at his knees. Alexandra looked back at Sheldon Smythe, but his large eyes were closed. The room was growing darker. Thunderstorm.

'I shall of course contest the will,' added Alexandra, 'if someone will allow me to see it.'

'But since you aren't mentioned in it,' said Sheldon Smythe, 'it is a document which bears no relevance to you. You are here by Mrs Linden's courtesy.'

'Gee, thanks,' said Alexandra. 'But Sascha must be mentioned, and I'm Sascha's mother.'

'Sascha's name appears nowhere on this document.'

'But I'm Ned's wife,' said Alexandra. 'And Sascha's Ned's child. I don't understand this.'

'Alexandra,' said Hamish, 'it so happens that I found Ned's marriage certificate to Pilar in his papers. We've checked it out. There's been no divorce, and Pilar is still alive. Ned's marriage to Chrissie, his subsequent divorce, his marriage to you, have neither legal meaning nor effect.'

'I told you,' said Jenny Linden to Dave. 'It wasn't adultery. Ned told me all about Pilar. Why didn't you believe me? I don't go with married men.'

Dave laughed and stopped holding his wife's hand. His white hair was damp with sweat. It curled around his face and made him look like an unhappy child at bathtime. His sleeves were rolled up; he wore no jacket. Still he was hot. Sheldon Smythe wore a suit but managed to look cool. Hamish wore a navy blazer with a handkerchief, Ned's favourite red-and-white-spotted handkerchief, neatly folded, perfectly creased, tucked into the breast pocket. Ned kept handkerchiefs to blow his nose on, not for decoration. He preferred them unironed. They were softer.

Alexandra supposed that Theresa, under Hamish's instructions, must have ironed the scrap of fabric, carefully stretched the bevelled hand-sewn edges, wrinkled from the washing machine, with the hot metal; folded exactly, passed, folded again, passed.

Theresa liked ironing. Alexandra had given Ned the handkerchief in the early years of their marriage. She was suddenly angry. Her house, her home, her very past, all picked over, ransacked. Turn your back for a moment, let down your guard, show yourself defenceless, and you could find yourself ethnically cleansed, betrayed by once friendly friends and neighbours greedy for what was yours: others lying in your bed, sitting in your chairs, looking out at your view, and yourself wandering homeless, nothing but a refugee. Toad in *The Wind in the Willows*, returning after a spell in prison to his family Hall, to find it noisy with carousing hostile stoats and weasels and himself barred entrance.

Alexandra said to Hamish, 'I suppose all this is because I wouldn't fuck you.'
Sheldon Smythe said, 'No bad language, please.'
Hamish said, 'It was my duty. I am obliged to disclose all evidence. These are legal matters.'

Jenny Linden said that poor Ned had been trying to sort out the Pilar business, no one was to blame him. He'd only been nineteen. He'd always thought it would somehow go away, but Leah had explained how life blessings needed transparency to shine through, and that Pilar was a shadow of opaqueness in his life. Once he'd been properly divorced from Pilar, he'd be in a position to marry her, Jenny.
'What about me?' asked Alexandra.
'You were bored with the relationship, it was obvious. Ned felt it. It really hurt him for a time. You'd be better on your own. You had your career. It was all that mattered to you.'
Sheldon Smythe coughed, and said should they all get on, he realised it was difficult for everyone.
Alexandra said to Jenny, 'Actually, Ned was the one to get bored. He was bored by you, irritated by you, did everything he could to get rid of you, but hell you were stubborn, complained to me about your smelly armpits, invited Abbie into his bed and double-booked, making sure you came round to get a good view.'

Jenny Linden screamed and leapt at Alexandra, but her husband caught her, pinioned her arms, and set her back in her chair. He was very strong, and a little manic. Alexandra felt a little surge of sexual response: it occurred to her that it would be quite fun to seduce him, Jenny Linden's husband, just for the hell of it. But that would be descending to their level.

Sheldon Smythe called in his secretary ostensibly to take notes, but perhaps because he felt he needed another witness; or an extra pair of arms in case someone else needed pinioning. Alexandra recognised her as Becky Witham to whom she'd taught drama at the local school. Couldn't move, couldn't act, but always helpful.
Alexandra gave a little laugh.

Alexandra said, 'Even so, folks, bigamously married or not, I have Ned's child. The courts will see me right.'
Jenny Linden shrieked. 'Bitch! That's not Ned's child. That brat is Eric Stenstrom's child, everyone knows. You foisted him on poor Ned. You are the foulest woman in the world. No wonder you didn't come to the funeral.' Dave Linden twisted her wrists, and she yelped.

There was silence. Sheldon Smythe opened a file which lay on his desk. In it were letters in Ned's handwriting: the ones on top quite fresh, the ones below on yellowed paper. The top one started, 'Dear Hamish.'
'So you weren't lying,' said Alexandra to Hamish.
'I never lie,' said Hamish.
'You don't take after your fucking brother, then,' she said. 'Perhaps your mother did get out one night.'
Hamish advised Alexandra to behave, she was going to be in considerable need of his help in future.

'In a letter here to his brother,' said Sheldon Smythe, 'Mr Ludd writes to say he believes that you, Mrs Ludd, are pregnant by a man other than himself; the Mr Stenstrom Mrs Linden refers to. Mr Ludd was obviously very distressed.'

Jenny Linden was calm again. She even apologised.

'Leah says Kali is very strong in me. I'm a conductor for male as well as female currents. I should be sorry for you, Alexandra, I pass through anger and out the other side. It's just you wasted so many of Ned's years.'

Jenny Linden turned to her husband and looked up at him with moist and gentle eyes. He loosed his grip on her arm: he raised one of her hands to his lips and kissed it, as if in apology. Jenny Linden directed a triumphant glance at Alexandra, as if to say, 'All this and a man too!'

'Problem is,' said Alexandra, 'you only have to look at Sascha to know he's Ned's child.'

'Eric Stenstrom is very much the same physical type as Ned and myself,' said Hamish. 'We're all old Aberdeen family: Viking stock.'

'Thank you, Hamish,' said Alexandra.

'It does rather seem to be your type, Alexandra,' said Hamish.

'Ned was scarcely cold and Alexandra was already making advances to poor Hamish,' said Jenny Linden to Sheldon Smythe. 'She was dancing about in front of him naked.'

Alexandra didn't deign to reply. She was like Brer Rabbit with the Tar Baby. The more she struggled the tighter she would get stuck. She should not have come here on her own. She should have brought a lawyer. She contented herself with saying, 'Ned acknowledged Sascha as his own, he's named on the birth certificate, and Ned supported him. That's enough for any sensible person.'

'But Ned did not acknowledge him as his own, you were the one who registered the birth, and you have done all the earning since the child was born according to Mr Hamish Ludd here.'

'Thank you, Mr Hamish Ludd,' said Alexandra.

'Sometimes I think she's on drugs,' said Jenny Linden. 'She's so frivolous. She has no idea how distressed Ned was about her being pregnant by another man. She's just completely self-centred. She can't bear to hear the truth spoken.'

'Mr Ludd left the child nothing in his will,' Mr Smythe observed.

'Which a court would find significant. Had you been legally married, your child would have a claim on the estate, as would you, whether Ned was the genetic parent or not. As the marriage is bigamous, the question of paternity is certainly relevant. Of course we'll have to take counsel's opinion, and you can fight the will through the courts by all means, if you can afford to, but so far as I can see nothing stands between my client Mrs Linden and her inheritance.'

'Except justice,' said Alexandra, 'common sense and tissue-typing.'

There was a short silence.

'You can't tissue-type from ashes,' said Hamish.

'You shouldn't have had Ned cremated,' said Jenny Linden. 'Serves you right.'

Alexandra saw Ned walking up his hill through the forest. It was dark, and the trees set closely together. It was almost impossible to find a path. She could only just see his back through the fog. No wonder he hadn't looked back. That was probably better than this.

'Poor Alexandra,' said pudgy little Jenny Linden, kindly, 'all this must come as a shock to her.' She spoke to her husband.

'I didn't mean to fall in love with Ned,' she said. 'He put some kind of spell on me. I was obsessed for a time, but it's over now. I'm glad we've been able to talk it all out properly, in a group like this. I wish Leah could have been here. She would have been proud of us. And Ned did the decent thing in the end, Dave, he left me the home. We must treasure it and look after it, in his memory. Ned liked you, Dave. He never said a word against you.' Becky Witham's eyebrows were raised: she was trying not to meet Alexandra's eye.

'There'd have to be a lot of changes made,' said Dave, 'before I'd consent to live in that morgue of a place. It would have to be brought up to date. My sound systems can't stand too much dust. All that would be expensive.'

'We can always sell off some of the antiques,' said Jenny.

Alexandra stood up.

'Will someone section this woman under the Mental Health Act? Fetch the men in white coats?'

'That earthenware Dog of Fo,' said Jenny, taking no notice, 'that white sort of blob with mad eyes, is worth £7,500. Ned told me so.'

'It used to be "ours",' said Alexandra. 'So now presumably it's mine. What are you talking about?'

'I know it's difficult for you to take this in, Alexandra,' said Hamish. 'As difficult as it was for Chrissie, once upon a time. I was very fond of Chrissie. I looked after her for a time, when Ned was finished with her.'

'Poor Hamish,' murmured Alexandra. 'What it is to be a younger brother. All you ever get is left-overs.'

Sheldon Smythe coughed. He had taken out another folder: this one was of blue cellophane. He said that Mr Ludd had bequeathed the contents of the house to Mrs Linden, as well as the house itself. He, Sheldon Smythe, understood that these included antiques of considerable value.

'I was able to trace receipts for most of the good stuff,' said Hamish, 'here and there in the muddle. All of them were made out in my brother's name only, and were paid for out of his bank account, not the joint account.'

'But I was the one who put money into Ned's account,' said Alexandra. 'His royalties had drifted away to almost nothing.'

'That was your choice,' said Hamish, bleakly. 'You can't give money away and then say what's bought with it is yours.'

'Ned hated the way she gave him money,' said Jenny Linden. 'He said Alexandra used money in all sorts of ways, to control, and manipulate, and buy love, but mostly, Leah says, to ease her guilt, because of Sascha.'

Sheldon Smythe said it was doubtful that Alexandra Ludd could persuade a court that the contents of The Cottage were matrimonial property, in spite of her having cohabited with Mr Ludd for years. But she must see her own lawyer.

Jenny Linden smiled. It seldom happened, but when she did her face lit up. Alexandra could see what Ned saw in her. Perhaps she looked like that when he and she were love-making. A transformation of Ned's making: ascent of the Holy Ghost; in triumph and elation both. Saving graces!

She asked Sheldon Smythe when the will had been made. Hamish asked if that was a proper question. Sheldon Smythe said he saw no reason for secrecy. Mr Ludd had made the will some three years ago. Alexandra said she expected he'd have been in soon enough to change Jenny Linden's name to Abbie Carpenter. Like musical beds when the music stopped, whoever was in the right one got to unwrap the parcel. Jenny Linden stopped smiling and glowered.

34

Alexandra left Sheldon Smythe's office and walked the three miles home. The temperature had dropped suddenly. It was noon but the sky was dark. There were specks of rain in the air: the wind had got up. She had goose pimples on her bare arms. Thunder cracked in the distance. Worst fears. She thought perhaps the answer to worst fears might not, after all, be high hopes but best wishes. High hopes could be dashed; best wishes simply remain. The world turned on a pin; it kept sticking: you needed to help it along.

Alexandra offered her best wishes to Ned. She could see he was badly in need of them. She could not offer him forgiveness, since there was no such thing. Best wishes she could manage. If Ned had believed Sascha was not his son, if Ned believed the betrayal was hers, Alexandra's, then he was not so much to blame: she must have appeared as hateful to him as he had lately to her. More fool he that he had let Jenny Linden persuade him of it, more tragic for him, and her, Alexandra, that he had died believing it. A sore point in the universe which could never heal: a wound forever open. Pitiful that a proper love could be so fragile, so easily undermined, but how could she, Alexandra, have hoped to make up, single-handedly, for a childhood which, if it produced Hamish, had produced Ned as well? She was naive and self-important to have thought she could.

Good times while they lasted, that was the most she could say, hurling best wishes after Ned, into the heart of the forest, where he wandered, lost in limbo. She was sure he was lost. It was too dark for him. But now she could see him. A lightning flash all around her, all around Ned too, lighting his way. Best wishes. Four seconds between thunder and lightning. The storm was four miles away. She called Ned's name. He turned and saw her and smiled. A dream but not a dream. You did not sleep as you walked home, trying to put your life in order, a life now in total disarray.

Best Wishes. She was elated. That was the secret: Best Wishes.

A car pulled in and drew up in front of her. It was a three-mile walk from Eddon Gurney to The Cottage. The road wound between high banks and trees which sometimes met overhead. It was a pretty walk, but long. Abbie was driving the car, on her way back from the supermarket to Elder House.
'Everything OK?' she asked.
'Just fine,' said Alexandra.
'Want a lift?'
'Yes,' said Alexandra. She got in. A tractor was about to overtake Abbie's car. Abbie pulled out without checking to see if anything was coming. They missed a collision by a fraction of an inch.
'These people never look,' complained Abbie, turning round to make faces at the tractor driver, who was Kevin Crump, and swerved over to the wrong side of the road. An approaching van was obliged to pull over to his right to avoid her and in his panic smacked into the tractor.
'Serve him right,' said Abbie, and continued driving. 'It was only a little bang,' she said, confidently, after they were safely round a bend and out of sight.
'No one will have got hurt. People ought to drive more slowly on these country roads.'
She told Alexandra she should have gone to Ned's funeral. It was too bad of her. 'Your own husband. People will think you have no feelings.'
'I don't have many left,' said Alexandra. 'I couldn't spare any for a cremation, and social chit-chat.'
'There was lots of that,' said Abbie. She described the funeral in detail and said that Ned had been a very popular man.
'Was "Sailing By" your idea?' Abbie asked.

'Yes.'

'It sounded ridiculous,' complained Abbie.

'As in life so in death,' said Alexandra.

'Talking about the ridiculous,' Abbie said, she'd seen the photograph of Jenny Linden in the paper and the caption 'Alexandra Ludd mourns' beneath. Things could hardly get more absurd.

'So long as no one thinks that's what I look like,' said Alexandra, offended.

'You're so vain,' said Abbie.

'And you're so treacherous,' said Alexandra, with a savagery that startled them both. 'You're lucky I haven't killed you. But you'll kill yourself soon enough with your own driving, so why should I bother.'

'But you'll trust Sascha to me,' said Abbie, 'to drive him to school and back every day because that suits you.'

That silenced Alexandra. The road in front was dark; they drove through twilight but the clock on the dashboard said it was lunchtime. The road carved through a hillside, and went through woods. Alexandra thought she might see Ned stumbling out into the road. All woods were probably alive with the accursed dead, against whom the living had grievances.

'Sorry,' she said to Abbie. 'I'm all over the place.'

'You certainly are,' said Abbie. 'If it's any consolation to you Ned and I were just sitting in the bed, wondering whether to or whether not to, and would probably have decided not to, out of loyalty to you, when Jenny came in, and he grabbed his chest, and so on, like people do in films.'

'How did you get to be sitting in the bed in the first place?'

'We'd been watching *Casablanca* and got bored. I used to find talking to Ned difficult. Ned made me feel inadequate, you know? So I'd prattle on about plum jam and he'd despise me even more. If you're having sex you don't need to talk so much. It's something to do.'

'I suppose it is,' said Alexandra. 'Shall we not talk about it?'

Abbie asked Alexandra how she'd got on at the lawyer's.

Alexandra said that for some reason Ned had left everything to Jenny Linden.

Abbie said no wonder Alexandra was in such a bad temper, and

Ned was a fool. He must have done it when he was sulking about something or other Alexandra had done, or not done, like come home, and then forgotten to revoke it. Alexandra would just have to go to court and do it herself. Alexandra said there were circumstances which might make that difficult. Abbie said Ned had certainly not been best pleased to see Jenny Linden when she came into the room dressed in a black and scarlet suspender belt and white lace stockings and nothing else, and his ashes were around to prove it.

'After he died she took his toothbrush,' said Alexandra.

'And the socks he'd been wearing that day,' said Abbie. 'Can you imagine?'

A wind had got up, presage of the storm, which still did not break. Great boughs tossed above their heads. The road finally took them out of the wood, and to the crossroads, and the left turn which took them to The Cottage.

As the car turned down the drive, the sun glinted out through a rent in the black clouds, and the day was suddenly bright again.

'Creepy weather,' said Abbie.

'Very suitable,' said Alexandra, pushing open the gate. It jangled gently as it always did when moved. Ned had attached some ancient animal bell to it, as an early-warning system against visitors. Loud enough to be heard at a distance, soft enough not to startle the animals. She wondered how often Jenny Linden had pushed it, heard it, contemplated the anticipatory excitement that would go with it. Worst Fears. She and Jenny were in some international war; Jenny winning: pushing forward, taking territory, defiling memory, altering history. Now she, Alexandra, must retreat. But she would adopt a scorched-earth policy. You had to be careful though; you had to do it on purpose, not by accident, and you could not allow yourself any possibility of return. Napoleon's army had got it wrong in the autumn of 1812, stripping the countryside bare as it went, raping and looting, emptying the brimming barns, killing the fat livestock, advancing like locusts. But winter came and there was no one to declare the glory of victory or the martyrdom of defeat. Napoleon's army

187

had to crawl home through the starved landscape it had itself created, dying by the hundred thousand of hunger, cold and disgrace. If you scorched earth you must bar the way to your own retreat. Well, that was OK.

'Blowing up a storm,' said Abbie.

The leaves of the Virginia creeper were beginning to turn red around their finely formed, delicate edges. Four weeks from now the stone walls would seem to be on fire. The house always looked good this time of year.

'Quite a wind,' said Alexandra. It whipped her ears and shivered up her skirt. It was exhilarating. There was no such thing as a defeat, if you didn't accept it.

The sun went beneath a serrated layer of black cloud; most of the light went with it. Inside the house Diamond lay back his ears and whimpered, very much preferring outside to in, and began to scrabble at the back door.

'It's OK, Diamond,' Alexandra called to him. 'It's only a storm.'

Alexandra and Abbie pushed and pushed at the door, but it didn't open. There was damp in the air: sometimes the door would stick after a long spell of hot weather. Alexandra had a vision of herself in a future which would be hers if she allowed it to be. It was as in the dream she had at Angliss Street. She was shut out, standing outside in the cold, beating against the locked back door. 'Let me in, let me in!' she was crying; Jenny's little face peered at her through the window; she knew Ned was in there but he didn't come to look. He was blind and deaf to her existence: he might as well be dead. The body in the morgue had been the metaphor: this dream, this vision, was the reality. Jenny was going about her business in her, Alexandra's, home; at her table with her, Alexandra's, erstwhile friends; preparing food, opening wine, pouring tea, victorious. Hamish would be a regular guest, she could foresee it. She was the ghost, they were living flesh and blood. She was the one who haunted her own home; the one Diamond saw, why Diamond crept under the table. Alexandra pushed and pushed on the door, in her vision; and then Ned pushed too. He wasn't on the inside, he never had been, he was on the outside with her, Alexandra, with her and Diamond, and against Jenny. Ned recognised Alexandra again. He had made a dreadful mistake. She, Alexandra, must put it right. She had not been to the funeral; that ceremony was trivial. There must be a proper funeral pyre. He demanded it.

The door opened suddenly; Alexandra and Abbie went in. There was no Jenny, just the familiar hall, and the dining room where Ned had not died, and the bright rugs on the polished floor, and an instant warmth, once out of the wet, cool wind: and a stillness, an emptiness. Everything was very quiet: the house waited for a decision from its keeper. Even the ghosts were still, acquiescent. What was going to be must happen.
'So still, out of the wind!' said Abbie, sensing something, but not sure what. Diamond went to lie beneath the kitchen table.

Jenny Linden had circled the borders and massed her forces, and pounced, and now cried 'Mine!' but it wasn't so. Couldn't be. Best wishes, Ned! I hope you had a happy time. I hope you made her glow. Life's short.

'You OK?' asked Abbie.
She was making tea in the kitchen.
'Fine,' said Alexandra. 'It's so grim out there,' she said. 'I'll just light a little fire to cheer ourselves up.'
'Good idea,' said Abbie.

The house insurance was in both their names: Ned's and hers. The payments came out of Ned's bank account, into which she, Alexandra, paid money. Ned paid the bills, looked after the paperwork of the household, in a desultory fashion. She supposed he had renewed the policy. It did not matter. Money was not the point.

Alexandra went out to fetch firelighters and logs from the barn. Twigs crackled beneath her feet. Everything was bone-dry. The

189

storm might carry with it the first signs of moisture for weeks, but the rain had not begun in earnest. Just a heavy drop or so, wind carried, quickly evaporating. She stood on the path and watched the wind whip away the bean-pole pyramids Ned had built: the bean plants writhed and stretched and reached into the air before falling. They seemed alive.

Alexandra went back into the house with her basket of logs, and lugged them not into the living room, but into the dining room. Hamish, in his search for documents, the better to incriminate her, Alexandra, the better to destroy her, had littered the grate in here with piles of old envelopes, papers, the recorded trash of the past. Alexandra saw an old school report of her own, despised and discarded by Hamish, and left it where it lay. Why bother? Who wanted anything of so sorry a past, so much of it based upon vanity and indecision? The shelf above the grate was all but hidden by cards – postcards from friends, invitations for Private Views, antique fairs, First Nights, P R junkets, Sascha's drawings. More of Sascha's drawings Blu-Tacked casually to the wall above, edges curling: just a little leap across for a flame, and on to the parched curtains; another leap and the flame would be over to bookcases: and the hundreds of art cards collected over years, propped up against books.
'Where's our book on early porcelain, Ned?' 'Behind the Picasso, you know, the geometric lady.' 'Where's the biographical encyclopaedia, Alexandra?' 'Behind the Monet, you know, those dozy water lilies, I think. Somewhere near Van Gogh's boots.'

The crows – or was it jackdaws? – built their nests in the dining room chimney. For some reason they scorned the chimney tha led up from the living room. Sweep the chimney as you would the new vacuum method of chimney-sweeping never quite gc rid of the twigs. Masses of them. They stuck and clung in th crevices of the sooty bricks. You'd have to send children uj said Ned, if you wanted this chimney really swept. Sometimes collection of tangled sticks would fall through into the gra with a bang and a great puff of dust, soot and ancient bird sl

Each single twig in its time had been lovingly carried by some trusting bird to an entirely inappropriate nesting place. Dangerous for fledglings. Alexandra and Ned never lit the fire in the dining room, for the young birds' sake. Who could tell what family dramas went on up there? But it was nearly autumn. The young ones should all have flown the nest by now. Dave Linden and Jenny would convert, modernise, remove fireplaces and chimneys altogether. Fireplaces mean dust, and fire.

Alexandra arranged paper, firelighter, twigs and logs in the grate, making a neat pyramid, decorous, but perhaps a little too large for its iron nest. She applied a match to the paper.
'Sorry,' she said, to anyone or anything which was listening, and felt the house prepare itself.

'That'll soon warm us up!' she called out to Abbie, and went into the kitchen for tea. Abbie settled in to tell Alexandra more about the funeral. Abbie was conscious of the frozen peas she had bought thawing in the back of her car, but said nothing about them. She was doing her best for her friend, who smiled a lot but seemed distracted.

Soon Alexandra heard a roaring noise coming from the dining room. A whoosh, an echo, and a steady, windy, throaty noise continuing after.
'Listen to the wind,' she said. 'How it's getting up.'
'So it is,' said Abbie. 'Howling round the chimneys.'
'Abbie,' said Alexandra, 'could we leave the house right now? Drive over to your place? Hamish might come back and I really don't want to see him. I couldn't face it! Or even Jenny Linden, to say how we can all be friends, or her husband Dave to marvel at how I ever got by in this kitchen.'
'OK,' said Abbie, 'if you're sure you don't want to finish your tea. It seems a waste to me.'
'I want to go now,' said Alexandra. 'And it's got so peculiar in here. Look how Diamond's trembling.'
'Old houses always move and shift,' said Abbie, 'and make

strange noises. You've got so much imagination, when it comes to things that don't matter.'

But Abbie got up from her chair and they left the kitchen together, and Alexandra went into the dining room for a moment as they left, careful to stay between Abbie and any sight of what was happening to the far wall.

'Fire OK?' asked Abbie as they went out of the back door. Diamond shot out ahead of them.

'Fire's fine,' said Alexandra. 'I threw an extra log on.' And so she had.

Sparks hurled themselves into the blue-black sky from the dining-room chimney. Spitter-spat of raindrops. Fire and rain must fight it out. Abbie didn't look up to see them. The wind howled. Abbie and Alexandra had to lean into it to get to the car. The rain was fitful. They hardly got wet.

Diamond chased them up to the top of the drive, barking.

'Hang on a minute,' said Alexandra, and Abbie stopped the car. Alexandra opened the door and Diamond trod her into the seat with desperate paws, clambering through to the back.

At the top of the drive they came nose to nose with Jenny Linden's little car. Abbie had to break suddenly to manoeuvre by, and managed to stall her engine. Hamish was driving. Jenny Linden sat next to him. Dave and Sheldon Smythe sat in the back. They gawped out of the windows at Alexandra. She waved cheerily.

'All yours!' she mouthed, but she didn't think they understood. She could see The Cottage in the side mirror. There was most certainly a chimney fire, and flickers of light running up and down the east side of the house, which might well be flames. It was a pity the others had arrived so soon. She could have done with an extra ten minutes. All it would have needed.

There was a sudden hammer-blow of thunder and a brilliant flash of lightning, zig-zagging down from above. For a second it turned all their faces blue as corpses. It seemed there'd been a direct hit on The Cottage. Now the roof too was aflame: fire raced over the tiles, burning what? Old leaves, wooden beams, who was to say? Flames were now coming out of the side window downstairs, too: marvellous, melodramatic red light reflected back from the clouds.

'Divine intervention sometimes comes when it isn't needed,' said Alexandra. 'Shall we get going?'

The occupants of the other car mouthed and shouted. Abbie, distracted, put the car into reverse gear and drove sharply backwards into the other vehicle, blocking the entrance to the drive. No one was hurt: all were shaken; everyone got out and stood staring down at The Cottage. The wind whipped through the building from east to west, as windows cracked and broke; it carried flame upstairs to the bedrooms while the flame from upstairs travelled down. What a fire that was, devouring Ned's papers, Ned's clothes, twisting and blackening the frame of the brass bed; gnawing through the linen cupboard, charring the split ammonite so no one now would ever recognise it for what it was; shattering the crystal, making a nonsense of the settle, the Picasso, the refectory table; what price now all the polishing, the dusting? All gone. Only the fireback (1705), would survive this, rather more blackened than usual, but with its golden lads and lasses still surviving, still dancing through the disasters of the centuries. Everything else gone. All Sascha's toys; everyone's school reports, photographs of ancient relatives, grandmother's love letters, books, books, books, more books. CDs would melt. Tears went up in steam. Ghosts fled. Ned's house, never hers, like Ned, gone to embers, gone to ashes. The house wanted it. The rain held off.

Sparks got to the barn. If the house went, how could the barn remain? Its thatched roof burst into a thousand flames. The wind roared. Everything in there went: from the wooden handles of the antique tools that should have gone to the Folk Museum but never did, to the bits and pieces of old furniture waiting for ever for restoration. What price now, all that weight of conscience, the burden of things undone that should have been done: better everyone had just partied while they could. The fire brigade bulldozed Abbie and Jenny's cars to one side, to allow them access. They made short work of them. Water from the hoses made the whole hillside smell like damp flesh and burnt dinner for days. There were no hydrants so far from civilisation. Ingeniously, the firemen drained the pond so the ducks were homeless, but the wind was too strong for them to do much about anything; they let the fire burn itself out, then simply damped everything down.

Arthur, on Abbie's hysterical return in a police car, was glad there was no loss of life.

Vilna cried for the newts, sucked up from the pond by the firemen's hoses.

Mr Quatrop rejoiced. Where there was a fire, there would later be development. The firemen said they suspected first a chimney fire – old crows' nests were always a hazard – compounded by a lightning strike. Alexandra shared her guilt with God, which meant she felt none. The insurance company declined to pay up. Ned had not paid the last instalment due. A final reminder had come with the condolence letters, and been overlooked. Insurance companies are not moved by personal tragedy: they have seen too many.

Gone. Worst fears. Along with them, Alexandra's clothes, books, papers, past. Alexandra's family photos, documentations, school reports, love letters from Ned. And others, kept hidden. Alexandra's pots, pans, plates, cups, saucers, sheets: things used and abused by Jenny Linden. 'She walked in when you walked out.' So who wanted them?

Alexandra's cosmetics, favourite eyeshadows, mementoes from past shows. Gifts from friends. A suspender belt in black and crimson that didn't fit. Alexandra's address book and diary, and Jenny Linden's too. Except Jenny Linden had her own copy. Pity. Like losing your handbag but a hundred times worse. Alexandra had taken her purse up when she left with Abbie just before the fire.

'Strange,' Abbie had thought at the time, but didn't care to pursue the thought thereafter. Too dangerous. A chimney fire compounded by a lightning strike. An act of god.
Gone, Ned, with Alexandra's blessing.

Hamish took the ashes back to Scotland.

A neat navy-blue cardboard box, rather heavy.

35

Alexandra called her mother and said now she, Alexandra, was homeless, could she leave Sascha there by the golf course, with the kittens, where he was happy? She knew her mother to be a careful driver. She called Eric Stenstrom and said could he look in on Sascha every now and then, and gave him the address. Every good child deserves a father. She called the man from Amblin and said she would take the part. Yes, she would play opposite Michael Douglas. You bet.

She called the theatre. She wasn't going to argue about not going back to *A Doll's House*, she wasn't going to sue: let Daisy Longriff bare her breasts every night. Best wishes, Daisy! Since apparently management had expected her, Alexandra, to do that very thing, should they be obliged to accept her return to the part, they on their side had broken the terms of her contract, so goodbye. She was on her way to Hollywood.

Alexandra stayed with Vilna in the meantime. But declined to share Vilna's bed. She gave Diamond to Kevin Crump: Diamond would be happy with a proper occupation, herding cows to the milking sheds. Kevin Crump had a broken arm following a hit-and-run accident with the tractor, but was now engaged to Sheldon Smythe's secretary, and was happy.

Alexandra best-wished everyone on her departure. Ned, again, and Abbie, and even Leah, and Vilna, and Arthur, and Dave Linden; Dr Moebius, and Mr Quatrop, and even Hamish, who kept calling and writing with remorse and apologies and whom she could not be bothered to despise or dislike, and Theresa, who, on hearing about the fire, instantly returned such of Alexandra's treasures as she had taken – offering them as gifts, of course: the Belgian lace tablecloth, the Arts and Crafts fire-tongs, the birdcage and the glass bowl. She best-wished Mr Lightfoot, and Mrs Paddle and even Chrissie, and her mother, and her mother's husband, whose name she had forgotten, and Sascha, and Sascha with all her heart, weeping but doing it, leaving her child because everyone was right on that subject. Sometimes grandmothers are better than mothers, with children. Best-wishing.

She could not best-wish Sheldon Smythe, he was not worth it, and she could, but would not, best-wish Jenny Linden. She must be allowed some indulgence, some caprice. And she best-wished Ned again, because what was the point of not? Ned was dead. And she was off.